Nora R ... hor
of more ... n
storyteller, sh ... umour and
poignancy that speaks directly to her readers and has
earned her almost every award for excellence in her
field. The youngest of five children, Nora Roberts lives in
western Maryland. She has two sons.

Visit her website at www.noraroberts.com.

Nora Roberts

The Winning Hand

Silhouette and Colophon are registered trademarks of
Harlequin Books S.A., used under licence.

First published in Great Britain ... House, 18–24 Paradise Road,
... 1SR

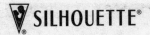

All the characters in this book have no existence outside the imagination
of the author, and have no relation whatsoever to anyone bearing the same
name or names. They are not even distantly inspired by any individual
known or unknown to the author, and all the incidents are pure invention.

CITY OF LONDON LIBRARIES	
CL 1117864 7	
HJ	10-Dec-2010
GENERAL	£6.99
FICTION	DD

Silhouette and Colophor
Harlequin Books S.A., u
Silhouette Books, Eton
Richmond, Surrey TW9

© Nora Roberts 1998

ISBN: 978 0 263 88937

026-1210

Silhouette Books' policy is to use papers that are
natural, renewable and recyclable products and made from
wood grown in sustainable forests. The logging and
manufacturing processes conform to the legal environmental regulations
of the country of origin.

Printed in the UK
by CPI MacKays, Chatham, ME5 8TD

To the Vegas Queens, with thanks

THE MACGREGORS

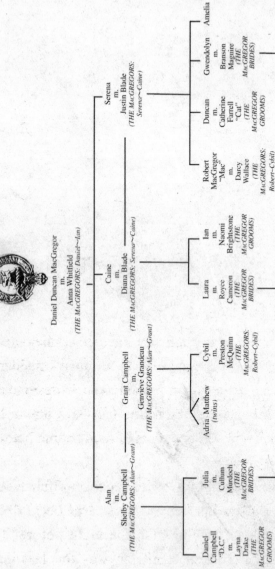

Daniel Duncan MacGregor
m.
Anna Whitfield
(THE MacGREGORS: Daniel~Ian)

Alan
m.
Shelby Campbell
(THE MacGREGORS: Alan~Grant)

Grant Campbell
m.
Genviève Grandeau
(THE MacGREGORS: Alan~Grant)

Caine
m.
Diana Blade
(THE MacGREGORS: Serena~Caine)

Serena
m.
Justin Blade
(THE MacGREGORS: Serena~Caine)

Daniel Campbell "D.C."
m.
Layna Drake
(THE MacGREGOR GROOMS)

Julia
m.
Cullum Murdoch
(THE MacGREGOR BRIDES)

Travis

Fiona Joy

Adria Matthew
(twins)

Cybil
m.
Preston McQuinn
(THE MacGREGORS: Robert~Cybil)

Laura
m.
Royce Cameron
(THE MacGREGOR BRIDES)

Ian
m.
Naomi Brightstone
(THE MacGREGOR GROOMS)

Daniel

Blake

Robert MacGregor "Mac"
m.
Darcy Wallace
(THE MacGREGORS: Robert~Cybil)

Duncan
m.
Catherine Farrell "Cat"
(THE MacGREGOR GROOMS)

Gwendolyn
m.
Branson Maguire
(THE MacGREGOR BRIDES)

Amelia

Ethan

Anna

Lauren

Chapter One

When her car sputtered and died a mile outside of Las Vegas, Darcy Wallace seriously considered staying where she was and baking to death under the brutal desert sun. She had 9.37 left in her pocket and a long stretch of road behind her that led to nowhere.

She was lucky to have even that pitiful amount of cash on her, as her purse had been stolen outside a diner in Utah the night before. The rubbery chicken sandwich was the last meal she'd had, and she figured the stray ten she'd found in her pocket was the last miracle she could expect.

Both her job and her home in Kansas were gone. She had no family and no one to go back to. She felt she'd had every reason for tossing her clothes into a suitcase and driving away from what had been, and what would have been, had she remained.

She'd driven west simply because her car had been pointing in that direction and she'd taken it as a sign. She'd promised herself an adventure, a personal odyssey and a new, improved life.

Reading about plucky young women who braved the world, carved a path, took risks and blithely accepted challenges was no longer enough. Or so she'd told herself as the miles had clicked away on the odometer of her ancient and sickly sedan. It was time to take something for herself, or at least to try.

If she had stayed, she would have fallen in line. Again. Done what she was told. Again. And spent her life haunted by dreams and regrets.

But now, one long week after sneaking out of town in the middle of the night like a thief, she wondered if she was destined for the ordinary. Perhaps she'd been born to follow all the rules. Maybe she should have been content with what life offered and kept her eyes cast down, instead of constantly trying to peek around the next corner.

Gerald would have given her a good life, a life she knew many women would envy. With him, she could have had a lovely home tidily kept by a loyal staff, closets bursting with conventionally stylish wife-of-the-executive clothes, a summer place in Bar Harbor, winter getaways to tropical climes. She would never be hungry, never do without.

All it required was for her to do exactly as she was told, exactly when she was told. All it required was for her to keep buried every dream, every longing, every private wish.

It shouldn't have been hard. She'd been doing it all of her life.

But it was.

Closing her eyes, she rested her forehead on the steering wheel. Why did Gerald want her so much? she wondered. There was nothing special about her. She had a good mind and an average face. Her own mother had described her just that way often enough. She didn't believe it was so much a physical attraction on Gerald's side, though she suspected he liked the fact she was a small woman of slight build. Easily dominated.

God, he frightened her.

She remembered how furious he'd been when she'd cut off her shoulder-length hair, snipping away until it was as short as a boy's.

Well, she liked it, she thought with a little spurt of defiance. And it was her hair, damn it, she added, pushing her fingers through choppily cut, toffee-colored locks.

They weren't married yet, thank the Lord. He had no right to tell her how to look, how to dress, how to behave. And now, if she could just hold on, he never would have that right.

She should never have agreed to marry him in the first place. She'd just been so tired, so afraid, so confused. Even though the regrets and the doubts had set in almost immediately, even though she'd given him back the ring and apologized, she might have gone through with it rather than stand up under his anger and live through the gossip of a broken engagement. But she'd discovered he'd manipulated her, that he was responsible for her losing her job, for the threat of eviction from her apartment.

He'd wanted her to buckle. And she'd nearly obliged him, she thought now as she wiped sweat from her face with the back of her hand.

The hell with it, she decided and pushed herself out of the car. So she had less than ten dollars, no transportation and a mile hike ahead of her. She was out from under Gerald's thumb. She was finally, at twenty-three, on her own.

Leaving her suitcase in the trunk, she grabbed the weighty tote that contained all that really mattered to her, then headed off on foot. She'd burned her bridges. Now it was time to see what was around that next corner.

It took her an hour to reach her destination. She couldn't have explained why she kept walking along Route 15, away from the scatter of motels, gas stations, and toward that shimmering Oz-like skyline of Vegas in the distance. She only knew she wanted to be there, inside that globe of exotic buildings and shapes where lights were twinkling like a carnival.

The sun was tipping down below the western peaks of the red mountains that ringed that glittering oasis. Her hunger had gone from grinding distress to a dull ache. She considered stopping for food, to rest, to drink, but there was something therapeutic about simply putting one foot in front of the other, her eyes on the tall, spectacular hotels glimmering in the distance.

What were they like inside? she wondered. Would everything be glossy and polished, colorful to the point of gaudy? She imagined an atmosphere of sex and gambling, desperation and triumph, with an underlying snicker of naughtiness. There would be men with hard eyes, women with wild laughs. She'd get a job in one of those opulent dens of indulgence and have a front row seat for every show.

Oh, how she wanted to live and see and experience.

She wanted the crowds and the noise, the hot blood and the cold nerves. Everything, everything that was the opposite of what she'd had before. Most of all she wanted to feel—strong, ripping emotions, towering joys, vivid excitement. And she would write about it all, she determined, shifting the tote which, filled with her notebooks and manuscript pages, weighed like stone. She would write, tucked in some little room looking out at it all.

Stumbling with exhaustion, she tripped on a curb, then righted herself. The streets were crowded, everyone seemed to have somewhere to go. Even at dusk, the lights of the city winked and gleamed and beckoned: *Come in, take a chance, roll the dice.*

She saw families of tourists—fathers in shorts with legs pink from the unforgiving sun, children with wide eyes, mothers with the frantic look of sensory overload.

Her own eyes were wide, the golden brown glazed with fatigue. The man-made volcano erupted in the distance, drawing screams and cheers from the crowd who'd gathered to watch and making Darcy gape with glassy-eyed wonder. The noise smothered the odd buzzing in her ears as she was jostled by the crowd.

Dazed and dazzled, she wandered aimlessly, gawking at the huge Roman statues, blinking at the neon, passing by the spurting fountains that gushed with shifting colors. It was a wonderland, loud and gaudy and unapologetically adult, and she was as lost and as fascinated as Alice.

She found herself standing in front of twin towers as white as the moon and joined together by a wide, curved bridge with hundreds of windows. Surrounding the building were seas of flowers, both wild and exotic, and pools of mirror-bright water fed by the rush of a terraced waterfall that tumbled from the topmost spear of a mountain.

Guarding the entrance to the bridge was an enormous—five times larger than life—Indian war chief astride a gold stallion. His face and bare chest were gleaming copper. His war bonnet flowed with winking stones of rich reds and blues and greens. In his hand he carried a lance with a diamond-bright tip that winked fire.

He's so beautiful, was all she could think, so proud and defiant.

She would have sworn the statue's dark eyes

were alive, fixed on hers. Daring her to come closer, to go inside, to take her chances.

Darcy stepped into The Comanche on watery legs and swayed against the sudden rush of cool air.

The lobby was immense, the tile floors a bold geometric pattern of emerald and sapphire that made her head spin. Cacti and palms grew regally out of copper or pottery urns. Brilliant floral displays graced huge tables, the scent of the lilies so sweet it brought tears to her eyes.

She walked on, amazed by the waterfall that rushed down a stone wall into a pond filled with bright fish, the sparkling light that shimmered from huge crystal-and-gold chandeliers. The place was a maze of color and flash, brighter and more brilliant than any reality she'd known or any dream she'd imagined.

There were shops, the offerings in the windows as glittery as the chandeliers. She watched an elegant blonde debate between two diamond necklaces the way another might consider her choice of tomatoes.

A laugh bubbled up in Darcy's throat, forcing her to press a hand to her mouth to hold it in. It wasn't the time or place to be noticed, she warned herself. She didn't belong in such glamorous surroundings.

She turned the corner and felt her head reel at the sudden brassy sound of the casino. Bells and voices, the metallic rat-a-tat of coins falling on coins. Whirls and buzzes and hoots. The wave of energy pouring out brought a rush to her blood.

Machines were everywhere, shoulder to shoulder with their faces spinning with colors and shapes. People crowded around them, standing, sitting on stools, pulling coins from white plastic buckets and feeding the busy machines. She watched a woman press a red button, wait for the spin to end, then scream with delight as triple black bars lined up in the center. Money poured out into a silver bowl in a musical rush.

It made Darcy grin.

Here was fun, reckless and impulsive. Here were possibilities both grand and small. And life, loud, messy and hot.

She'd never gambled in her life, not with money. Money was something to be earned, saved and carefully watched. But her fingers slipped into her pocket where the last of her crumpled bills seemed to pulse with heat against her skin.

If not now, when? she asked herself with another bubbling giggle she could no longer quite control. What good was 9.37? It would buy her a meal, she told herself, gnawing on her lip. But then what?

Light-headed, her ears ringing oddly, she roamed the aisles, blinking owlishly at people and machines. They were willing to take a chance, she thought. That's why they were here.

Wasn't that why she was here?

Then she saw it. It stood alone, big and bright and fascinating. It stood taller than she, its wide face made up of stylized stars and moons. The handle was nearly as thick as her arm and topped with a shiny red ball.

It called itself Comanche Magic.

JACKPOT! it proclaimed in diamond-white lights that flashed on and off and made her dizzy. Ruby red dots flowed along a black strip. She stared, fascinated at the number showing within the blinking lights.

1,800,079.37

What an odd amount. Nine dollars and thirty-seven cents, she thought again, fingering the money in her pocket. Maybe it was a sign.

How much did it cost? she wondered. She stepped closer, blinked to clear her wavering vision and struggled to read the rules. It was a progressive machine, so the numbers would change and grow as players pumped in their money.

She could play for a dollar, she read, but that wouldn't get the jackpot even if she lined up the stars and moons on all three lines. To really play, she'd have to put in one dollar times three. Nearly all the money she had left in the world.

Take a chance, a voice seemed to whisper slyly in her ear.

Don't be foolish. This voice was prim, disapproving, and all too familiar. *You can't throw your money away.*

Live a little. There was excitement in the whisper, and seduction. *What are you waiting for?*

"I don't know," she muttered. "And I'm tired of waiting."

Slowly, her eyes on the challenging face of the machine, Darcy dug into her pocket.

* * *

With his gaze scanning the tables, Robert Mac-Gregor Blade scrawled his initials on a chit. The man in chair three on the hundred-dollar table wasn't taking his losses in stride, he noted. Mac lifted a brow as the man held on fifteen with the dealer showing a king. If you're going to play for a hundred a hand, he mused as the dealer turned up a seven, you ought to know how to play.

In a casual gesture, Mac lifted a hand to call over one of the tuxedoed security men. "Keep an eye on him," Mac murmured. "He's thinking about making trouble."

"Yes, sir."

Spotting trouble and dealing with it was second nature for Mac. He was a third-generation gambler, and his instincts were well honed. His grandfather, Daniel MacGregor, had made a fortune taking chances. Real estate was Daniel's first love, and he continued to buy and sell property, to develop and preserve, to wheel and deal, though he was into his nineties.

Mac's parents had met in a casino aboard ship. His mother had been dealing blackjack, and his father had always been a player. They'd clashed and they'd clicked, both initially unaware that Daniel had maneuvered their meeting with marriage and the continuation of the MacGregor line in mind.

Justin Blade had already owned The Comanche in Vegas, and another in Atlantic City. Serena MacGregor had become his partner, then his wife.

Their eldest son had been born knowing how to roll the dice.

Now, just shy of his thirtieth birthday, Comanche Vegas was his baby. His parents trusted him enough to leave it in his hands, and he made very certain they wouldn't regret it.

It ran smoothly because he made certain it ran smoothly. It ran honest because it always had. It ran profitably because it was a Blade-MacGregor enterprise.

He believed, absolutely, in winning—and always in winning clean.

His lips twitched as a woman at one of the five-dollar tables hit twenty-one and applauded herself. Some would walk away winners, Mac mused, most wouldn't. Life was a gamble, and the house always had the edge.

A tall man, he moved through the tables easily, in a beautifully tailored dark suit that draped elegance over tough and ready muscle. The legacy from his Comanche heritage showed in the gold-dust skin pulled tight over his cheekbones, in the rich black hair that framed a lean, watchful face and flowed to the collar of his formal jacket.

But his eyes were Scot blue, deep as a loch and just as unfathomable.

His smile was quick and charming when a regular hailed him. But he kept moving, barely pausing. He had work waiting in his office high above the action.

"Mr. Blade?"

He glanced over, stopping now as one of the roving cocktail waitress moved to him. "Yes?"

"I just came over from the slots." The waitress shifted her tray and tried not to sigh as Mac gave her the full benefit of those dark blue eyes. "There's a woman over at the big progressive. She's a mess, Mr. Blade. Not too clean, pretty shaky. She might be on something. She's just staring at it, you know? Muttering to herself. I thought maybe I should call security."

"I'll take a look."

"She's, well, she's kind of pathetic. Not a working girl," the waitress added. "But she's either sick or stoned."

"Thanks, I'll take care of it."

Mac shifted directions, moving into the forest of slots rather than his private elevator. Security could handle any trouble that threatened the smooth operation of the casino. But it was his place, and he handled his own.

A few feet away, Darcy fed her last three dollars into the slot. You're insane, she told herself, carefully babying the last bill when the machine spit it back at her. You've lost your mind, her pounding heart seemed to scream even as she smoothed the bill and slid it back in. But God, it felt so good to do something outrageous.

She closed her eyes a moment, breathing deeply three times, then opening them again, grabbed the shiny red ball of the arm with a trembling hand.

And pulled.

Stars and moons revolved in front of her eyes,

colors blurred, a calliope tune began to jingle. She found herself smiling at the absurdity of it, almost dreaming as the shapes spun and spun and spun.

That was her life right now, she thought absently. Spinning and spinning. Where will it stop? Where will it go?

Her smile only broadened as stars and moons began to click into place. They were so pretty. It had been worth the price just to watch, to know at least she'd pulled the handle.

Click, click, click, shining stars, glowing moons. When they blurred, she blinked furiously. She wanted to see every movement, to hear every sound. Wasn't it pretty how neatly they all lined up? she thought and braced a hand against the machine when she felt herself begin to tip.

And as she touched it, as her hand made contact with the cool metal, the movement stopped. The world exploded.

Sirens shrieked, making her stagger back in shock. Colored lights went into a mad dance atop the machine, and a war drum began to beat. Whistles shrilled, bells clanged. All around her people began to shout and shove.

What had she done? Oh God, what had she done?

"Holy cow, you hit the big one!" Someone grabbed her, danced with her. She couldn't breathe, flailed weakly to try to escape.

Everyone was pushing, pulling at her, shouting words she couldn't understand. Faces swam in front of hers, bodies pressed until she was trapped against the machine.

An ocean was roaring in her head, a jackhammer pounded in her chest.

Mac moved through the celebratory crowd, nudging well-wishers aside. He saw her, a slip of a woman who looked barely old enough to be inside the casino. Her dark blond hair was short and messily cut, bangs flopping down into enormous fawn colored eyes. Her face was angular as a pixie's and pale as wax.

Her cotton shirt and slacks looked as though she'd slept in them, and as if she'd spent her sleeping hours curled up in the desert.

Not stoned, he decided when he took her arm and felt the tremble. Terrified.

Darcy cringed, shifted her gaze to his. She saw

the war chief, the power and the challenge and the romance of him. He'd either save her, she thought dizzily, or finish her.

"I didn't mean—I only…what did I do?"

Mac angled his head, smiled a little. A dim bulb, perhaps, he mused, but harmless. "You hit the jackpot," he told her.

"Oh, well, then."

She fainted.

There was something wonderfully smooth under her cheek. Silk, satin, Darcy thought dimly. She'd always loved the feel of silk. Once she'd spent nearly her entire paycheck on a silk blouse, creamy white with tiny gold buttons, heart-shaped buttons. She'd had to skip lunch for two weeks, but it had been worth it every time she slipped that silk over her skin.

She sighed, remembering it.

"Come on, all the way out."

"What?" She blinked her eyes open, focused on a slant of light from a jeweled lamp.

"Here, try this." Mac slipped a hand under her head, lifted it and put a glass of water to her lips.

"What?"

"You're repeating yourself. Drink some water."

"Okay." She sipped obediently, studying the tanned, long-fingered hand that held the glass. She was on a bed, she realized now, a huge bed with a silky cover. There was a mirrored ceiling over her head. "Oh my." Warily she shifted her gaze until she saw his face. "I thought you were the war chief."

"Close." He set the glass aside, then sat on the edge of the bed, noting with amusement that she scooted over slightly to keep more distance between them. "Mac Blade. I run the place."

"Darcy. I'm Darcy Wallace. Why am I here?"

"It seemed better than leaving you sprawled on the floor of the casino. You fainted."

"I did?" Mortified, she closed her eyes again. "Yes, I guess I did. I'm sorry."

"It's not an atypical reaction to winning close to two million dollars."

Her eyes popped open, her hand grabbed at her throat. "I'm sorry, I'm still a little confused. Did you say I won almost two million dollars?"

"You put the money in, you pulled the lever, you hit." There wasn't an ounce of color in her cheeks, he noted, and thought she looked like a bruised fairy. "We'll deal with the paperwork when you're feeling a little steadier. Do you want to see a doctor?"

"No, I'm just…I'm okay. I can't think. My head's spinning."

"Take your time." Instinctively he plumped up the pillows behind her and eased her back. "Is there someone I can call to help you out?"

"No! Don't call anyone."

His brow lifted at her quick and violent refusal, but he only nodded. "All right."

"There isn't anyone," she said more calmly. "I'm traveling. I—my purse was stolen yesterday in Utah. My car broke down a mile or so out of town. I think it's the fuel pump this time."

"Could be," he murmured, tongue in cheek. "How did you get here?"

"I walked in. I just got here." Or she thought she had. It was hard to remember how long she'd walked around, goggling at everything. "I had nine dollars and thirty-seven cents."

"I see." He wasn't sure if she was a lunatic or a first-class gambler. "Well, now you have approximately one million, eight hundred thousand, eighty-nine dollars and thirty-seven cents."

"Oh…oh." Shattered, she put her hands over her face and burst into tears.

There were too many women in his life for Mac to be uncomfortable with female tears. He sat where he was, let her sob it out.

An odd little package, he thought. When she'd slid unconscious into his arms she'd been limp as water and had weighed no more than a child. Now she'd told him she'd hiked over a mile in the stunning late spring heat, then risked what little money she'd had on a yank of a slot.

That required either steel or insanity.

Whichever it was, she'd beaten the odds. And now she was rich—and for a while at least, his responsibility.

"I'm sorry." She wiped at her somehow charmingly dirty face with her hands. "I'm not like this. Really. I can't take it in." She accepted the handkerchief he offered and blew her nose. "I don't know what to do."

"Let's start with the basics. When's the last time you ate?"

"Last night—well, I bought a candy bar this morning, but it melted before I could finish it. So it doesn't really count."

"I'll order you some food." He rose, looking down at her. "I'll have them set it up down in the parlor. Why don't you take a hot bath, try to relax, get your bearings."

She gnawed her lip. "I don't have any clothes. I left my suitcase in my car. Oh! My bag. I had my bag."

"I have it." Because she'd gone pale again, he reached down beside the bed and lifted the plain brown tote. "This one?"

"Yes. Yes, thank you." Relief had her closing her eyes and struggling to calm herself again. "I thought I'd lost it. It's not clothes," she added, letting out a long sigh. "It's my work."

"It's safe, and there's a robe in the closet."

She cleared her throat. However kind he was being, she was still alone with him, a perfect stranger, in a very opulent and sensual bedroom. "I appreciate it. But I should get a room. If I could have a small advance on the money, I can find a hotel."

"Something wrong with this one?"

"This what?"

"This hotel," he said with what he considered admirable patience. "This room."

"No, nothing. It's beautiful."

"Then make yourself comfortable. Your room's comped for the duration of your stay—"

"What? Excuse me?" She sat up a little straighter. "I can have this room? I can just... stay here?"

"It's the usual procedure for high rollers." He smiled again, making her heart bump. "You qualify."

"I do?"

"The management hopes you'll put some of those winnings back into the pot. At the tables, the shops. Your room and meals, your bar bills, are on us."

She eased off the bed. "I get all this for free, because I won money from you?"

This time his grin was quick, and just a little wolfish. "I want the chance to win some of it back."

Lord, he was beautiful. Like the hero in a novel. That thought rolled around in her jumbled brain. "That seems only fair. Thank you so much, Mr. McBlade."

"Not McBlade," he corrected, taking the hand she offered. "Mac. Mac Blade."

"Oh. I'm afraid I haven't been very coherent."

"You'll feel better after you've eaten, gotten some rest."

"I'm sure you're right."

"Why don't we talk in the morning, say ten o'clock. My office."

"Yes, in the morning."

"Welcome to Las Vegas, Ms. Wallace," he said, and turned toward a sweep of open stairs that led to the living area.

"Thank you." She ordered her shaky legs to carry her to the rail, then lost her breath when she looked down at the sprawling space done in sapphires and emeralds, accented with ebony wood and lush arrangements of tropical flowers. She watched him cross an ocean of Oriental carpet. "Mr. Blade?"

"Yes?" He turned, glanced up, and thought she looked about twelve years old and as lost as a lamb.

"What will I do with all that money?"

He flashed that grin again. "You'll think of something. I'd make book on it." Then pressing a button, he stepped through the brass doors that slid open, into what surely was a private elevator.

When the doors closed again, Darcy gave in to her buckling knees and sat on the floor. She hugged herself hard, rocked. If this was some dream, some hallucination brought on by stress or sunstroke, she hoped it never cleared away.

She hadn't just escaped, she realized. She'd been liberated.

Chapter Two

The bubble didn't burst in the morning. She shot awake at six o'clock and stared, startled, at her reflection in the mirror overhead. Testing, she lifted a hand, watched herself touch her cheek. She felt her fingers, saw them slide up over her forehead and down the other side of her face.

However odd, it had to be real. She'd never seen herself horizontal before. She looked so…different, she decided, sprawled in the huge, rumpled bed surrounded by a mountain of pillows. She felt so different. How many years had she awakened each morning in the practical twin bed that had been her nesting place since childhood?

She never had to go back to that.

Somehow that single thought, the simple fact that she would never again have to adjust her body to the stingy mattress of the ancient bed sent a rush of joy through her so wild, so bright she burst into giddy laughter, unable to stop until she was gasping for air.

She rolled from one end of the bed to the other, kicked her feet in the air, hugged pillows, and when that wasn't enough, leaped up to dance on the mattress.

When she was thoroughly winded, she dropped down again and wrapped her arms tight around her knees. She was wearing a silk sleep shirt in candy pink—one of several articles of basic wardrobe that had arrived just after her dinner. Everything had been from the boutique downstairs and had been presented to her courtesy of The Comanche.

She wasn't even going to worry about the fact that the gorgeous Mac Blade had bought her underwear. Not when it was such fabulous underwear.

She jumped up, wanting to explore the suite again. The night before, she'd been so punchy she'd just wandered around gawking. Now it was time to play.

She snatched up a remote and began punching buttons. The shimmering blue drapes over the floor-to-ceiling windows opened and closed, making her grin like a fool. Opening them again, she saw she had a wide window on the world that was Vegas.

It was all muted grays and blues now, she noted, with a soft desert dawn breaking. She wondered how many floors up she was. Twenty? Thirty? It hardly mattered. She was on top of a brave and very new world.

Choosing another button, she opened a wall panel that revealed a big-screen television screen, a VCR and a complicated-looking stereo system. She fiddled until she filled the room with music, then raced downstairs.

She opened all the drapes, smelled the flowers, sat on every cushion of the two sofas and six chairs. She marveled at the arched fireplace, at the grand piano of showy white. And because there was no one to tell her not to touch, she sat down and played the first thing that came into her mind.

The celebratory, arrogant notes of "Everything's Coming Up Roses" made her laugh like a loon.

Behind a glossy black wet bar she found a small refrigerator, then giggled like a girl when she saw it contained two bottles of champagne. With the music blaring, she waltzed into the bath off the living area and grinned at the bidet, the phone, the wall-mounted TV and all the pretty toiletries arranged in a china basket.

Humming to herself, she climbed the curving chrome steps back to the bedroom. The master bath was a symphony of pure sensory indulgence from the lake-sized motorized tub in sensuous black to the acre of counter under a wall-sized lighted mirror. The room was bigger than her entire apartment back home.

Tuck in a bed, she thought, and she could live happily right here. Lush green plants lined the tiled shelf beside the tub. A separate rippled glass shower stall offered crisscrossing sprays. Lovely clear jars were arranged on glass shelves and held bath salts, oils, creams with scents so lush she moaned in pleasure at every sniff.

The adjoining dressing room boasted a walk-in closet that contained a robe and a pair of brushed cotton slippers with The Comanche logo, a triple-glass, full-length mirror, two elegant chairs and a table where fragrant flowers spilled out of a crystal vase.

It was the kind of indulgence she'd only read about or seen in movies. Plush, sleek, shimmering with wealth. Now that her initial rush of adrenaline was leveling, she began to wonder if there hadn't been some mistake.

How could this have happened? The time and circumstances after she'd begun her long hike into town were all blurry around the edges in her mind now. Snatches of it came clear, the whirling lights on the machine, her own thumping heart, Mac Blade's impossibly handsome face.

"Don't question it," she whispered. "Don't ruin it. Even if it all goes away in an hour, you have it now."

Biting her lip, she picked up the phone and punched in the button for room service.

"Room service. Good morning, Ms. Wallace."

"Oh." She blinked, looking guiltily over her shoulder as if someone had sneaked up behind her. "I was wondering if I could order some coffee."

"Of course. And breakfast?"

"Well." She didn't want to take advantage. "Perhaps a muffin."

"Will that be all?"

"Yes, that would be fine."

"We'll have that up to you within fifteen minutes. Thank you, Ms. Wallace."

"You're welcome, um, thank you."

After she hung up, Darcy hurried into the bedroom to turn off the stereo, switch the TV on and check the news to see if there were any reports of mass hallucinations.

In his office above the carnival world of the casino, Mac flicked his gaze over the security screens where people played the slots, bet on red or waited for their dealer to bust. There were more than a few diehards who'd started the night before and were still going at it. Slinky evening dresses sat hip to hip with jeans.

Ten o'clock at night, ten in the morning, it made no difference. There was no real time in Vegas, no dress code, and for some, no reality beyond the next spin of the wheel. Mac ignored the whine of an incoming fax, sipped his coffee and paced the room as he spoke to his father on the phone.

He imagined his father was doing virtually the same thing in the office in Reno.

"I'm going to talk to her in a few minutes," Mac continued. "I wanted to let her smooth out a little."

"Tell me about her," Justin requested, knowing his son's instincts for people would give him a clear picture.

"I don't know a lot yet. She's young." He kept moving as he talked, watching the screens, checking on the placement of his security people, the attitude of the dealers. "Skittish," he added. "Looked like a woman on the move to me. Trouble somewhere. She's out of her element here."

He cast his mind back, bringing the image of Darcy into focus, letting himself hear her voice again. "Small-town, Midwest, I'd say. Makes me think of a kindergarten teacher—the kind the kids would love and take merciless advantage of. She was broke and running on fumes when she hit."

"Sounds like it was her lucky day. If someone's going to hit, it might as well be a broke, small-town kindergarten teacher."

Mac grinned. "She apologizes all over herself. Nervous as a mouse at a feline convention. She's cute," he said finally, thinking of those big, dark gold eyes. "And I'd have to guess naive. The wolves are going to tear off pieces of her in short order if she doesn't have some protection."

There was a short pause. "You planning on standing between her and the wolves, Mac?"

"Just steering her in the right direction," Mac muttered, rolling his shoulders. His reputation in the family for siding with the underdog was inescapable. "The press is already hammering at the door. The kid needs a lawyer, and some straight talk, because the vultures circle right after the wolves."

He imagined the barrage of requests and demands that would come, begging for contributions, offering investments. A smattering of them would be genuine, and the rest would be playing one of the oldest games. Get the money and run.

"Keep me up to date."

"I will. How's Mom?"

"She's good. Hosting some big charity fashion show here today. And she's making noises about dropping in on you before we head back East. A quick visit," Justin added. "She misses the baby."

"Uh-huh." Mac had to grin. He knew very well his father would crawl over broken glass for a chance to visit his grandchild in Boston. "So how is little Anna?"

"Great. Just great. She's teething. Gwen and Bran aren't getting a lot of sleep right now."

"The price you pay for parenthood."

"I had plenty of all-nighters with you, pal."

"Like I said…" Mac's grin widened. "You pay your money, you make your choice." He glanced up at the quiet knock on his door. "That must be the nervous fairy now."

"Who?"

"Our newest millionaire. Come in," he called out, then curled a finger when Darcy hesitated on the threshold. "I'll keep you posted. Tell Mom I said hi."

"I've got a feeling you can tell her face-to-face in a few days."

"Good. Talk to you later."

The minute he hung up, Darcy launched into an apology. "I'm sorry. I didn't realize you were on the phone. Your assistant, secretary, whatever, came to bring me up, and she said I should just come in. But I can come back. If you're busy…I can come back."

Patient, Mac waited until she'd run down. It gave him the opportunity to see what a meal and a good night's sleep had done for her. She looked a little less fragile, incredibly…tidy, he decided, in the simple blouse and slacks he'd had the boutique send to her suite. And no less nervous than the evening before.

"Why don't you sit down?"

"All right." She linked her fingers together, twisted them, then stepped to a high-backed deep-cushioned chair in hunter green leather. "I was wondering—thinking…has there been a mistake?"

The chair dwarfed her, and made him think of fairies again, perched on colorful toadstools. "Hmm? About what?"

"About me, the money. I realized this morning, when I could think a bit more clearly, that things like this just don't happen."

"They do here." Hoping to put her at ease, he leaned a hip on the corner of his desk. "You are twenty-one, aren't you?"

"Twenty-three. I'll be twenty-four in September. Oh, I forgot to thank you for the clothes." She ordered herself not to think about the underwear, not to so much as consider that *he* was thinking of it. But color rose into her cheeks. "It was very kind of you."

"Everything fit all right?"

"Yes." Her color deepened. The bra was a lovely champagne color with edgings of lace, and was precisely her size. She didn't want to speculate how he could have been quite so accurate. "Perfectly."

"How'd you sleep?"

"Like someone put me under a spell." She smiled a little now. "I suppose I haven't been sleeping well lately. I'm not used to traveling."

There was a dusting of freckles over her pert little nose, he noted, a paler gold than her extraordinary eyes. She smelled lightly of vanilla. "Where are you from?"

"A little town, Trader's Corners, in Kansas."

Midwest, Mac thought. Hit number one.

"What do you do in Trader's Corners, Kansas?"

"I'm—I was a librarian."

Close enough for hit number two, he decided. "Really? Why'd you leave?"

"I ran away." She blurted it out before thinking. He had such a beautiful smile, and he'd been looking at her as if he were really interested. Somehow he had lulled her into the admission.

He pushed away from the desk, then sat on the arm of the chair beside hers so that their faces were closer, their eyes more level. He spoke gently, as he might to a cornered puppy. "What kind of trouble are you in, Darcy?"

"I'm not, I would have been if I'd stayed, but..." Then her eyes widened. "Oh, I didn't do anything. I mean I'm not running away from the police."

Because she was so obviously distressed, he smothered the laugh and didn't tell her he couldn't imagine her getting so much as a parking ticket. "I didn't think that, but people generally have a reason for running away from home. Does your family know where you are?"

"I don't have any family. I lost my parents about a year ago."

"I'm sorry."

"It was an accident. A house fire. At night." She lifted her hands, dropped them into her lap again. "They didn't wake up."

"That's a lot to deal with."

"There was nothing anyone could do. They were gone, the house was gone. Everything. I wasn't home. I'd just moved into my own apartment a few weeks before. Just a few weeks. I…" She pushed absently at her fringe of bangs. "Well."

"So you decided to get away?"

She started to agree, to make it simple. But it wasn't the truth, and she was such a poor and guilty liar. "No. Not exactly. I suppose that's part of it. I lost my job a few weeks ago." It still stung, the humiliation of it. "I was going to lose my apartment. Money was a problem. My parents didn't have much insurance, and the house had a mortgage. And the bills." She moved her shoulders. "In any case, without a paycheck, I wasn't going to be able to pay the rent. I didn't have that much saved myself, after college. And sometimes I…I'm not very good with budgets, I suppose."

"Money's not going to be a problem now," he reminded her, wanting to make her smile again.

"I don't see how you can just give me almost two million dollars."

"You *won* almost two million dollars. Look." He took her hand, nudging her around until she could see the screens. "People step up to the tables, every hour, every day. Some win, some lose. Some of them play for entertainment, for fun. Others play hoping to make the big score. Just once. Some play the odds, some play a hunch."

She watched, fascinated. Everything moved in silence. Cards were dealt, chips were stacked, raked in or slipped away. "What do you do?"

"Oh, I play the odds. And the occasional hunch."

"It looks like theater," she murmured.

"That's what it is. With no intermission. Do you have a lawyer?"

"A lawyer?" The amused interest that had come into her eyes vanished. "Do I need a lawyer?"

"I'd recommend it. You're about to come into a large amount of money. The government's going to want their share. And after that, you're going to discover you have friends you've never heard of, and people who want to offer you a terrific opportunity to invest. The minute your story hits the press, they'll crawl out of the woodwork."

"Press? Newspapers, television? No, I can't have that. I can't have that," she repeated, springing up. "I'm not going to talk to reporters."

He bit back a sigh. Yes indeed, he thought, this one would need a hand to hold on the walk through the forest. "Young, orphaned, financially strapped librarian from Kansas walks into Comanche Vegas and drops her last dollar—"

"It wasn't my last," she insisted.

"Close enough. Her last dollar in the slot and

wins a million-eight. Darling, the press is going to do handsprings with a lead like that."

He was right, of course. She could see it herself. It was a wonderful story, just the kind she wanted to write herself. "I don't want it to get out. They have televisions and newspapers in Trader's Corners."

"Hometown girl makes good," he agreed, watching her. Suddenly he realized something else was putting panic into her eyes. "They'll probably name a street after you," he said casually.

"I don't want this to get back there. I didn't tell you everything." Because she had no choice but to hope he could help, she sat again. "I didn't tell you the main reason I left the way I did. There's a man. Gerald Peterson. His family's very prominent in Kansas. They own quite a bit of land and many businesses. Gerald, for some reason, he wanted me to marry him. He insisted."

"Women are still free to say 'no, thank you' in Kansas, aren't they?"

"Yes, of course." It seemed so simple when he said it, she mused. He would think she was an idiot. "But Gerald's very determined. He always finds a way to get what he wants."

"And he wants you," Mac prompted.

"Well, yes. At least he seems to think he does. My parents were very pleased that he was interested in me. I mean, who would think I'd catch the eye of a man like him?"

"Are you joking?"

She blinked. "What?"

"Never mind." He waved it away. "So Gerald wanted to marry you, and I take it you didn't want to marry him. What then?"

"A few months ago, I said I would. It seemed like the only reasonable thing to do. And he just assumed I would, anyway." Ashamed, she stared down at her linked fingers. "Gerald assumes very firmly. He doesn't hear the word no. It's like a genetic thing." She sighed. "Agreeing to marry him was weak, and stupid, and I regretted it immediately. I knew I couldn't go through with it, but he wouldn't listen when I tried to tell him. There was the whole ring thing, too," she added with a frown.

Fascinated and entertained, Mac cocked his head. "Ring thing."

"Well, it was silly, really. I didn't want a diamond engagement ring. I wanted something different, just…different. But he didn't hear that, either. I got a two-carat diamond, which was properly appraised and insured. He explained all about the investment value." She shut her eyes. "I didn't want to hear about the investment value."

"No," Mac murmured. "I don't imagine you did."

"I wasn't expecting romance. Well, no, yes I was, but I knew it wasn't going to happen. I thought I could settle." She looked past him, past the screens. "I should have been able to settle."

"Why?"

"Because everyone said how lucky I was. But I didn't feel lucky. I felt smothered, trapped. He was very angry when I gave him back the ring. He barely said a word, but he was furious. Then he wasn't. He was very calm and told me he had no doubt I'd come to my senses shortly. Once I did, we'd forget it had ever happened. Two weeks later, I lost my job."

She made herself look back at Mac. He was listening, she realized with some surprise. Really listening. Hardly anyone really listened. "They talked about budget cutbacks, my performance evaluation," she continued. "I was so shocked that it took me a little while to realize he'd arranged it. The Petersons endow the library. And they own my apartment building. He had to have known I'd come crawling back."

"Sounds to me like you gave him a good kick in the ass. Not as much as he deserved, but a solid shot."

"He'll be humiliated, and very, very angry. I don't want him to know where I am. I'm afraid of him."

Something new and icy flickered into Mac's eyes. "Did he hurt you?"

"No. Gerald doesn't have to use physical force when intimidation works so well. I just want to disappear for a while. He only wants me now because he can't tolerate being refused. He doesn't love me. I simply suit his needs in a wife. Neat, quiet, well educated and behaved."

"You'd feel better if you stood up to him."

"Yes." She lowered her gaze. "But I'm afraid I won't."

Mac considered a moment. "We'll do what we

can to keep your name out of it. The press should run with the mystery woman angle happily enough for a while. But it won't last, Darcy."

"The longer the better."

"Okay, let's deal with the basics. I can't distribute the money yet. You don't have any identification for one thing, and that makes it sticky. You'll need to get some. Your birth certificate, driver's license, that sort of thing. So we're back to a lawyer."

"I don't know any. Just the firm back home who handled things for my parents, and I wouldn't want to use them."

"No, they wouldn't do, not for a woman who wants to start a new life from scratch."

Her smile bloomed slowly, drawing his attention to the shape of her mouth, the full bottom lip, the deep dip centered in the top one. "I guess that's what I'm doing. I want to write books," she confessed.

"Really? What sort?"

"Love stories, adventures." She laughed and leaned back in the cushions of the chair. "Wonderful stories about people who do amazing things for love. I suppose that sounds crazy."

"It sounds rational to me. You were a librarian, so you must love books. Why not write them?"

She goggled first, then her eyes went bright and beautiful. "You're the first person I've ever told who's said that. Gerald was appalled at the very notion that I'd consider writing at all, much less romance novels."

"Gerald's an idiot," Mac said dismissively. "We've already established that. I guess you'd better buy yourself a laptop and get to work."

Staring again, she pressed a hand to her throat. "I could, couldn't I?" When her eyes began to fill, she shook her head quickly. "No, I'm not going to start that again. It's just that a life can change so completely and so quickly. The best and the worst. In a blink."

"You're handling this very well. You'll handle the rest." He rose and missed the startled look she shot him. No one had ever expressed such casual confidence in her before. "I'm not sure it's ethical, but I can contact my uncle. He's a lawyer. You can trust him."

"I'd appreciate it. Mr. Blade, I'm so grateful for—"

"Mac," he interrupted. "Whenever I give a woman almost two million dollars, I insist on a first-name basis."

Her laugh burst out, then was quickly muffled by her hand. "Sorry. It's just strange hearing that out loud. Two million dollars."

"A fairly amusing number," he said dryly, and her laughter stopped instantly.

"I never thought—I mean about your part. What it means to you, this place. You don't have to pay me all at once," she said in a rush. "It can be in installments or something."

On impulse he reached down, cupped her chin in his hand and studied her face. "You're incredibly sweet, aren't you, Darcy from Kansas?"

Her mind washed clean. His voice was so warm, his eyes so blue, his hand so firm. Her heart did one long, slow twist in her chest and seemed to sigh. "What did you say? I'm sorry?"

He skimmed his thumb over her jawline. Fairy bones, he thought absently, and catching himself wondering about her, he dropped his hand. Don't go there, Mac, he warned himself, and stepped back.

"The Comanche never makes a bet it can't afford to lose. And my grandfather doesn't really need that operation."

"Oh, God."

"I'm joking." More delighted with her than ever, he roared with laughter. "You're easy. Much too easy." They'll eat her alive, he thought. "Do yourself a favor, keep a low profile until my uncle starts the ball rolling. I'll advance you some cash."

He moved behind the desk and unlocked a drawer where he kept the petty cash. "A couple thousand should hold you. We've arranged for credit at the shops here for you. I imagine you'll want to make arrangements to have your car towed in." Expertly he counted out hundreds, then fifties.

"I'm having a little trouble breathing," Darcy said weakly. "Excuse me."

Mac glanced up, watched in some alarm as she lowered her head between her knees.

"I'll be all right in a minute," she told him when she felt his hand on the back of her head. "I'm sorry. I'm being an awful lot of trouble."

"No, but I'd definitely prefer it if you didn't faint again."

"I won't. I was just a little light-headed for a second." When the phone rang, she jolted, then sat straight up. "I'm taking too much of your time."

"Sit." He pointed, then snatched up the phone. "Deb, tell whoever it is I'll get back to them." He hung up again, narrowed his eyes and felt a genuine wave of relief that her color was back. "Better?"

"Much. I'm sorry."

"Stop apologizing. It's a very annoying habit."

"I'm—" She pressed her lips together, cleared her throat.

"Good." He picked up the stack of bills and handed it to her. "Go shopping," he suggested. "Go play. Get a massage or a facial, sit by the pool. Enjoy yourself. Have dinner with me tonight." He hadn't meant to say that, hadn't a clue where it had come from.

"Oh." He was frowning at her now, which was only more confusing. "Yes, I'd like that." Feeling awkward, she rose and pushed the bills into her pocket. She hadn't brought the lovely little shoulder bag the boutique had sent her, because she'd had nothing to put in it. "I don't know what to do first."

"It doesn't matter. Just do it all."

"That's a wonderful way of thinking." Unable to help herself, she beamed at him. "Just do it all. I'll try that. I'll let you get back to work." She started for the door, but he went to it with her and opened it. She looked up again, groping for the right words. "You saved my life. I know that sounds dramatic, but it's the way I feel."

"You saved it yourself. Now take care of it."

"I'm going to." She offered her hand, and because it was irresistible, he lifted it to his lips.

"See you later."

"Yes. Later." She turned and walked away without her feet touching the ground.

Mac shut the door, then dipping his hands into his pockets, stood staring at it. Darcy the Kansas librarian, he mused. Not his type. As far from his type as they came. The little pull he felt, he assured himself, was just concerned interest. Almost brotherly.

Almost.

It was the eyes that were doing it, he supposed. How was a man supposed to resist those big, wounded fawn eyes? Then there was the shy little hesitation in her voice followed by those quick bursts of enthusiasm. And the genuine sweetness of her. Nothing saccharine or cloying, just innocence, he supposed.

Which circled right back to the point. Not his type. Women were safer when they knew how to play the game. Darcy Wallace didn't have a clue.

Well, he couldn't very well hand her the money then toss her into the fray without a shield, could he?

Just steer her in the right direction, he promised himself, then wave goodbye.

With this in mind, he went back to his desk and picked up the phone. "Deb, get me Caine MacGregor's office in Boston."

Chapter Three

It was a different world. Perhaps even a different planet. And she, Darcy thought as she stepped cautiously into the sparkling boutique, was now a different woman.

The Darcy Wallace who so often had her nose pressed against the window of such pretty places was now inside. And she could have whatever she wanted. That gorgeous beaded jacket there, she thought—not daring to touch it—or that fluid column of ivory silk.

She could have them, both of them, all of them.

Because the world had turned upside down and somehow had shaken her out and dumped her right on top.

She stepped in a little farther, peeked into a long glass display cabinet. Beautiful, sparkly things. Foolishly wonderful decoration for ears and wrists and fingers. She'd always wanted to wear something that sparkled.

Odd, she'd never felt that special thrill she'd expected when she'd worn Gerald's ring on her finger. His ring, she realized now. Of course, that was it. It hadn't really been hers at all.

"May I help you?"

Startled, she looked up and nearly backed guiltily away from the display. "I don't know."

The woman behind the counter smiled indulgently."Are you looking for anything special?"

"Everything seems special."

The indulgent smile warmed. "I'm glad you think so. We're very proud of our selection. I'd be happy to help you if I can, or you can feel free to browse."

"Actually I have a dinner tonight, and nothing to wear."

"That's always the way, isn't it?"

"Literally nothing." When the clerk didn't appear especially shocked by this confession, Darcy drummed up the courage to go on. "I suppose I need a dress."

"Formal or casual?"

"I have no idea." Realizing the quandary, Darcy scanned the gowns and cocktail suits on display. "He didn't say."

"Dinner for two?"

"Yes. Oh." She turned back. "It's not a date. Exactly."

Willing to play, the clerk angled her head. "Business?"

"In a way. I suppose." She pushed at the hair that was tickling her ear. "Yes, that must be it."

"Is he attractive?"

Darcy rolled her eyes. "That doesn't begin to describe him."

"Interested?"

"You'd have to be dead ten years not to be. But it's not that sort of…thing."

"Maybe it could be. Let's see." Lips pursed, the clerk studied Darcy through narrowed eyes.

"Feminine but not fussy, sexy but not obvious. I think I have a few things you might like."

The clerk's name was Myra Proctor. She'd worked at the Dusk to Dawn Boutique for five years since she and her husband had moved to Vegas from Los Angeles. He was in banking, and she had worked in retail most of her adult life. She had two children, a boy and a girl. The girl had just turned thirteen and would surely make her mother's hair gray. Though, at the moment, Myra's hair was a sleek auburn.

Darcy learned all this because she asked. And asking helped put her at ease while Myra approved or rejected outfits.

One cocktail dress, beaded jacket, evening purse and sparkly earrings later, Myra gave her a gentle nudge toward the salon.

"You ask for Charles," Myra advised. "Tell him I sent you. He's an absolute genius."

"What," Charles demanded when Darcy sat in the cushioned silver salon chair, "happened to your hair? An industrial accident? A near-terminal illness perhaps? Mice?"

Wincing, Darcy cowered under the stark white cape that had been draped around her. "I'm afraid I cut it myself."

"Would you remove your own appendix?"

She could only hunch her shoulders as he glowered down at her with searing green eyes under dark, beetled brows. "No. No, I wouldn't."

"Your hair is a part of your body and requires a professional."

"I know. You're right. Absolutely." The back of her throat began to tickle and she swallowed gamely. It wasn't the time to laugh, however nervously, she reminded herself. Instead she tried an apologetic smile. "It was an impulse, a rebellion actually."

"Against what?" His fingers dove into her hair and began to knead and tug. "Being well-groomed?"

"No. Well…there was this man, and he kept telling me how I should wear it, and how it should be, and it made me mad, so I whacked it off."

"Was this man your hairdresser?"

"Oh, no. He's a businessman."

"Ha. Then he has no business telling you how

you should wear your hair. Cutting it off was brave. Foolish, but brave. The next time you want to rebel, go to a professional."

"I will." She took a deep breath. "Can you do anything with it?"

"My dear child, I've worked miracles with much worse." He snapped his fingers. "Shampoo," he ordered.

She'd never felt more pampered in her life. It was so beautifully indulgent to lie back, to have her hair washed, her scalp massaged, to listen to the birdlike murmurs of the shampoo girl. Even when she was back in Charles's chair, she felt none of the stomach-quivering anxiety that often rode hand in glove with a haircut.

"You need a manicure," Charles ordered, snipping away. "Sheila, squeeze in a manicure and pedicure for—what was your name, dear?"

"Darcy. A pedicure?" The thought of having her toes painted was so…exotic.

"Hmm. And you'll stop biting your nails immediately."

Chastised, Darcy tucked her hands under the cape. "It's a terrible habit."

"Very unattractive. You're fortunate, though. You have thick, healthy hair. A nice color. We'll leave that alone." He brought a section of hair up between two fingers, snipped. "What do you use on your face?"

"I have some moisturizer, but I lost it." Self-consciously she rubbed at her nose.

"The freckles are charming. You'll leave them alone, too."

"But I'd rather—"

"Are you picking up the scalpel?" he asked, arching one of his thick, black brows, then nodding, satisfied, when she shook her head. "I'm going to do your face myself. If you don't like the look, you don't pay. If you do like it, you not only pay, you buy the products."

Another gamble, Darcy thought. Maybe she was on a roll. "Deal."

"That's the spirit. Now…" He angled her head, snipped again. "Tell me about your love life."

"I don't have one."

"You will." He wiggled those eyebrows. "My work never fails."

By three, Darcy walked back into her suite. She was loaded down with purchases, and still floating. On impulse, she dumped everything on the sofa and dashed to the mirror. Myra had been right. Charles was a genius. Her hair looked pert, she decided with a chuckle. Almost sophisticated. Though it was even shorter than she had dared cut it, it was sleek and just a little sassy.

Her bangs didn't flop now, but spiked down over her forehead. And her face…wasn't it amazing what could be done with those tubes and brushes and powders? They couldn't make her a raving beauty, but she thought—she hoped—she'd stepped up to the threshold of pretty.

"I'm almost pretty," she said to her reflection, and smiled. "I really am. Oh, the earrings!" She whirled and dashed toward the bags, thinking the glitter against her face might just take her that final step.

Then she saw the red message light blinking on her phone.

No one knew where she was. How could any-one call her when no one knew? The press? Had the news gotten out already? No, no, she thought, clutching her hands together. Mac had promised not to give out her name. He'd promised.

Still her pulse hammered in her throat as she picked up the phone and pushed the message button. She was informed she had two new voice mail messages. The first was from Mac's assis-tant and had her releasing the breath she'd been holding. Mr. Blade would pick her up for dinner at seven-thirty. If that wasn't suitable, she had only to call back and reschedule.

"Seven-thirty is fine," she whispered. "Seven-thirty is wonderful."

The last message was from Caine Mac-Gregor, who identified himself as Mac's uncle and invited her to call him back at her conve-nience.

She hesitated over that. She found she didn't want to face the practical business of it all. Somehow it seemed much more romantic when it all remained dreamlike and impossible. But she'd been raised to return phone calls promptly, so she pulled out the chair at the desk, sat, and dutifully made the long-distance call to Boston.

When Darcy opened her door and found Mac holding a single white rose, she considered it another miracle. He was something out of one of the stories she'd secretly scribbled in notebooks for years. Tall, dark, elegantly masculine, heart-stoppingly handsome with just an edge of danger to keep it all from being too smooth.

The miracle was that he was there, holding out a long-stemmed rosebud the color of a summer cloud, and smiling at her.

But what popped out of her mouth was the single thought that had revolved in her muddled brain since her call to Boston.

"Caine MacGregor is your uncle."

"Yes, he is."

"He was attorney general of the United States."

"Yes." Gently Mac lifted Darcy's hand and placed the rose stem in it. "He was."

"Alan MacGregor was president."

"You know, I heard that somewhere. Are you going to let me in?"

"Oh. Yes. But your uncle, he was *president*," she said again, slowly, as if she'd been misunderstood. "For eight years."

"You pass the history quiz." Mac closed the door behind him and took a good long study of her. A warm hum of approval moved through his blood. "You look fabulous."

"I—really?" Distracted not only by the compliment, but the delivery, she glanced down. "I would never have chosen this," she began, running a hand over the copper-hued skirt of a dress that was shorter, snugger and certainly more daring than anything in her previous wardrobe. "Myra at the boutique, the evening wear boutique downstairs, picked it out. She said I belonged in jewel colors."

"Myra has an excellent eye." And likely deserved a raise, he thought, making a circling motion with his finger. "Turn around."

"Turn—" Her laugh was both pleased and self-conscious as she executed a slow twirl.

A big raise, Mac decided as the flippy little

skirt danced around surprisingly delightful legs. "They're not there."

"What?" Her hand fluttered to the dipping bodice, checking. "What isn't there?"

"Wings. I expected to see little fairy wings."

Flustered, she laughed again. "The way this day has gone, I wouldn't be surprised to see them myself."

"Why don't we have a drink before we go to dinner, and you can tell me how the day's gone?"

He walked to the bar to take a bottle of champagne out of the minifridge. She loved to watch him move. It was the animal grace she'd only read about, sleek and confident. And again, slightly dangerous. But to see it…she let out a little sigh. It was so much better than just imagining.

"Charles cut my hair," she began, thrilling to the celebratory sound of the cork popping.

"Charles?"

"In your salon?"

"Ah, that Charles." Mac selected two flutes from the glass shelves and poured. "The customers tremble, but always go back to Charles."

"I thought he was going to boot me out when

he saw what I'd done." She gave her short locks a tug. "But he took pity on me. Charles has definite opinions."

Mac skimmed his gaze over her hair, then down until his eyes met hers. "I'd say in your case he saw the wings."

"I'm only to pick up scissors to cut paper from now on." Her eyes danced as she accepted the glass Mac offered. "Or pay the consequences. And, if I bite my nails, I'll be punished. I was afraid to ask him how. Oh, this is wonderful," she murmured after a sip. Closing her eyes, she sipped again. "Why would anyone drink anything else?"

The pure sensual pleasure on her face had the hum in his blood quickening. A babe in the woods, he reminded himself. It seemed wiser all around to keep the bar between them. "What else did you do?"

"Oh, the salon took forever. Charles kept finding other things he said were absolutely essential. I had a pedicure." Humor danced into her eyes again. "I had no idea how wonderful it is to have your feet rubbed. Sheila put paraffin on my feet. Can you imagine? My hands, too. Feel."

He took the hand she held out, in all innocence. It was small and narrow, the skin as smooth as a child's. He had to check the urge to nibble. "Very nice."

"Isn't it?" Delighted with herself, Darcy smiled and stroked a finger over the back of her hand. "Charles said I have to have a full body loofah and some sort of mud bath, and…I can't even remember. He wrote it all down and sent me to Alice at the spa. She makes the appointments. I have to be there at ten—after I work out in the health club, because he believes I've been neglecting my inner body, too. Charles is very strict. May I have some more?"

"Sure." A little war between amusement and baffled desire waged inside him as he poured more champagne.

"This is a wonderful place. It has everything. Wonderful surprises around every corner. It's like living in a castle." Her eyes closed with pleasure as she drank. "I always wanted to. I'd be the princess under a spell. And the prince would scale the walls, tame the dragon—I always hated when they killed the dragon. They're so magical and magnificent. Anyway, once the prince came, the spell would be broken, and everything in the castle would come to life. The colors and the sounds. There'd be music and dancing. And everyone would be so happy. Ever after."

She stopped, laughed at herself. "The champagne's going to my head. This isn't at all what I wanted to talk to you about. Your uncle—"

"We'll talk about it over dinner." He slipped the flute from her hand and set it aside. He spotted the glittery little evening bag on a table and handed it to her.

She slanted him a look as he led her to the elevator. "Can I have more champagne at dinner?"

Now he had to laugh. "Darling, you can have whatever you want."

"Imagine that." With a blissful sigh, she leaned against the smoked glass wall.

He pushed the button for the circular restaurant on the top floor. She'd bought perfume, he thought, something woodsy and perfect for her. He decided the best place for his hands was in his pockets. "Did you try out the casino?"

"No. There was so much else to do. I looked around a little, but I didn't know where to begin."

"I think you began pretty well already."

She beamed up at him as the doors opened. "I did, didn't I?"

He led her through a small palm-decked foyer and into a candlelit dining room ringed by windows where silver gleamed against white linen.

"Good evening, Mr. Blade. Madam." The maître d' made a slight bow and, with his shoe-black hair and round body, reminded Darcy of Tweedledee of Alice fame.

Another rabbit hole, she thought as they were led to a curved banquette by the window. She never wanted to find her way out.

"The lady enjoys champagne, Steven."

"Of course. Right away."

"It must be so exciting living here. It's like a world to itself. You like it, don't you?"

"Very much. I was born with a pair of dice in one hand, and a deck of cards in the other. My mother and father met over a blackjack table. She was working as a dealer on a cruise ship, and he wanted her the minute he saw her."

"A shipboard romance." It made her sigh. "She was beautiful."

"Yes, she is beautiful."

"And he would have been dark and handsome, and maybe a little dangerous."

"More than a little. My mother likes to gamble."

"And they both won." Her lips tipped up, deepening the dip in the center. "You have a big family."

"Unwieldy."

"Only children are always jealous of big, unwieldy families. You're never lonely, I bet."

"No." She had been, he thought. There was no doubt of it. "Loneliness isn't an option." He nodded approval to the label as the sommelier offered the bottle of champagne.

Thrilled by the ritual, Darcy studied every step, the elegant spin of the white cloth, the subtle movement of the sommelier's hands, the muffled pop of cork. At Mac's signal, a small amount was poured into Darcy's glass for tasting.

"It's wonderful. Like drinking gold."

That earned her a pleased smile from the

sommelier, who finished pouring with a flourish before nestling the bottle in a silver bucket of ice.

"Now." Mac tapped his glass lightly against hers. "You talked with my uncle."

"Yes. I didn't realize, not until I'd made the call. Then I did—Caine MacGregor, Boston. I know I started to stutter." She winced. "He was very patient with me." A laugh bubbled up and was partially swallowed. "The former attorney general of the United States is my lawyer. It's so odd. He said he would take care of things—my birth certificate, the red tape. He didn't seem to think it would take very long."

"MacGregors have a way of moving things along."

"I've read so much about your family." Darcy accepted the leather-bound menu absently. "Your grandfather's a legend."

"He loves hearing that. What he is, is a character. You'd like him."

"Really? What kind of a character?"

How did one describe Daniel MacGregor? Mac wondered. "An outrageous one. Big, loud, bold. A Scotsman who built an empire on grit and sweat and shrewdness. He sneaks cigars—or my grandmother lets him believe he's sneaking them. He'll skin you at poker. Nobody bluffs better. He has an amazing heart, strong and soft. For him, family comes first and last and always."

"You love him."

"Very much." Because he thought she'd enjoy it, he told her of how a young, brash Daniel had come to Boston looking for a wife, had set his eyes on Anna Whitfield and, tumbling into love, had wooed and won her.

"She must have been terribly brave, becoming a doctor. There were so many obstacles for a woman."

"She's amazing."

"And you have brothers? Sisters?"

"One brother, two sisters, assorted cousins, nephews, nieces. When we get together it's…an asylum," he decided, making her laugh.

"And you wouldn't change it for the world."

"No, I wouldn't."

She opened her menu. "I always wondered what it would be like to—oh my. Look at all this. How does anyone decide what to order?"

"What do you like?"

She looked up, gold eyes sparkling. "Everything."

She sampled all she could manage. Tureen of duck, wild greens, little salmon puffs topped with caviar. Unable to resist, Mac scooped up some of his own stuffed lobster and held the fork to her lips. Her eyes closed, a quiet moan rippled in her throat, her lips rubbed gently together. And his blood flashed hot.

He'd never known a woman so open to sensual pleasure, or so obviously new to it. She'd be a treasure in bed, absorbing, lingering over every touch, every taste, every movement.

He could imagine it clearly—much too clearly—the little sighs and murmurs, the awakenings.

She gave one of those little sighs now as her long lids opened slowly over dreamy eyes. "It's wonderful. Everything's wonderful."

It was all flowing through her, mind and body, soft lights, strong flavors, the froth of wine and the look of him. She found herself leaning forward. "You're so attractive. You have such a strong face. I love looking at it."

From another woman it would have been an invitation. From her, Mac reminded himself, it was a combination of wine and naiveté. "Where do you come from?"

"Kansas." She smiled. "That's not what you meant, is it? I have no finesse," she confessed. "And when I relax, I tend to say things that pop into my head. I'm usually nervous around men. I never know what to say."

He arched a brow. "Obviously I don't make you nervous. That's my ego you hear thudding at your feet."

She chuckled, shaking her head. "Women are always going to fantasize about men like you. But you don't make me nervous, because I know you don't think of me that way."

"Don't I?"

"Men don't." She gestured with her glass before sipping. "Men aren't quickly attracted to women who aren't particularly physically appealing. Willowy blondes," she continued, eyeing his plate and wondering how to ask for another bite.

"Sultry brunettes, glamorous redheads. Attention focuses on them, it's only natural. And strongly attractive men are drawn to strongly attractive women. At least initially."

"You've given this a lot of thought."

"I like to watch people, and how they circle toward each other."

"Maybe you haven't looked closely enough. I find you very appealing, physically." He watched her blink in surprise as he slid a little closer. "Fresh," he murmured, giving in to the urge to cup a hand at the back of her slender neck. "And lovely."

He saw her gaze flit down to his mouth and return, startled, to his eyes. He heard the little rush of breath shudder through her lips. It was tempting, very tempting to close the slight distance, to complete the circle she'd spoken of. But she trembled under his hand, a trapped bird not entirely sure of her wings.

"There," he said quietly. "That shut you up. Nervous now?"

She could only move her head in short, rapid nods. She could all but feel his mouth on hers. It would be firm, and hot and so clever. The fingers at the back of her neck had stroked some wild nerve to life. She could feel it careen through her, bumping her pulse to light speed.

The dawning awareness in her eyes, the flicker of panic behind it had his fingers tightening briefly on her nape. "You shouldn't dare a gambler, Darcy." He gave her neck what he hoped was a friendly squeeze before easing back. "Dessert?"

"Dessert?"

"Would you like some?"

"I don't think I could." Not with her stomach muscles in knots and her fingers too unsteady to hold a fork.

He smiled slowly. "Want to try your luck?" When she swallowed, he added, "At the tables."

"Oh. Yes. I think I would."

"What should I play?" she asked him when they walked into the noise and lights of the casino.

"Lady's choice."

"Well." She bit her lip, tried to keep her mind

off the fact that he had his hand at the small of her back. It did no good to tell herself she had no business thinking of him that way. "Maybe black-jack. It's just adding up numbers, really."

He ran his tongue around his teeth. "That's part of it. Five-dollar table," he decided. "Until you get your rhythm." He led her toward a vacant chair in front of a dealer he knew to be both patient and personable with novices. "How much do you want to start with."

"Twenty?"

"Twenty thousand's a little steep for a beginner."

Her mouth dropped open, then curved on a laugh. "I meant dollars. Twenty dollars."

"Dollars," Mac said weakly. "Fine—if you think you can stand the excitement."

When he reached for his wallet, she shook her head. "No, I have it." She pulled a twenty out of her bag. "It feels more like mine this way."

"It is yours," he reminded her. "And at twenty, not a hell of a lot's going to be mine again."

"I might win." She slid onto a stool beside a portly man in a checked jacket. "Are you winning?" she asked him.

He tipped a beer to his lips and winked at her. "I'm up about fifty, but this guy." He gestured toward the dealer. "He's tough."

"You keep coming back to my table, Mr. Renoke," the dealer said cheerfully. "Must be my good looks."

Renoke snorted, then tapped his cards. "Give me a little one, pal."

The dealer turned up a four. "Your wish, my command."

"There you go." Renoke waved a finger over the cards to indicate he'd hold with nineteen. When the dealer held on eighteen, Renoke patted Darcy's shoulder. "Looks like you brought me some fresh luck."

"I hope so. I'd like to play," she added.

"Changing twenty," the dealer announced and shoved the bill into a slot with a clear plastic box. Darcy neatly stacked her four five-dollar chips. "Bets?"

"Put a chip on the outline there," Mac instructed.

The cards moved quickly, slipping out of the shoe and snapping lightly on felt. She was dealt a six and an eight, with the dealer showing ten.

"What do I do now?"

"Take a hit."

She tilted her head, looked up at Mac. "But I'm beating him, and a ten would put me over, wouldn't it?"

"Odds are his down card is over two. Play the odds."

"Oh. I'll take a hit." She pulled a ten, then frowned. "I lost."

"But you lost correctly," the dealer told her with a grin.

She lost correctly twice more and, with brows knit in concentration, slid her last chip into place. And hit blackjack. "I didn't even have to do anything." She wiggled more comfortably on the stool and sent Mac an apologetic look. "I think I'll play incorrectly for a while, just to see what happens."

"It's your game."

With some surprise, he watched her play against all logic and build her little stack of chips up to ten, dwindle them down to three, then build them back up again. She chatted with Renoke, learned about his two sons in college and neatly stacked her chips.

A twenty-dollar stake, he mused, and she was up to two hundred. The woman was a marvel.

He caught the eye of a dealer at another table, a subtle signal of trouble on the brew. "I'll be right back," he murmured to Darcy, giving her shoulder a light squeeze.

It wasn't hard to spot where the trouble was centered. The man in the first chair was down to three hundred-dollar chips. Mac judged him to be roughly forty, a little worse for liquor, and a poor loser.

"Look, you can't deal cleaner than that, you ought to be fired." The man jabbed a finger at the dealer while other players eased out of their chairs and looked for calmer water. "I can't win more than one hand out of ten. And that little bitch who was dealer before you's no better. I want some damn action here." He thumped his fist on the table.

"Problem?" Mac stepped up to the table.

"Back off. This is none of your damn business."

"It's my business." A subtle signal had his floor man, already moving toward the table, stopping. "I'm Blade, and this is my place."

"Yeah?" The man lifted his glass, gulped. "Well, your place is lousy. Your dealers think they're slick, but I can spot them." He slammed his glass down. "Bled me for three grand already. I know when I'm being taken."

Mac's voice remained low, his eyes cool. "If you want to lodge a complaint, you're welcome to do so. In my office."

"I don't have to go to your stinking office." In one violent gesture, he knocked his glass from the table. "I want some satisfaction here."

Mac held up a hand to hold off the two security guards who were moving rapidly in his direction. "You're not going to get it. I suggest you cash in and take your business elsewhere."

"You're kicking me out?" The man shoved away from the table. On his feet he wasn't steady, but he was big, burly and his fists were clenched. "You can't kick me out."

Ready violence flashed into Mac's eyes in a quick, icy flare. "Want to bet?"

Rage had the man trembling, visibly. But drunk or not, he recognized the cold fury staring him down. "The hell with it." He snatched up his chips, sneered. "I should've known better than to trust some Indian dive."

Mac's hand shot out like a lightning bolt, grabbed the man by the shirtfront and hauled his bulk onto his toes. "Stay out of my place." His voice was dangerously quiet, his eyes flat as ice. "I see you in here again, and you won't leave standing. Escort this…gentlemen to the cashier," Mac instructed his security team. "Then show him the door."

"Yes, sir."

"Half-breed son of a bitch," the man shouted as he was led away.

Mac's head jerked around when a hand touched his arm. Instinctively Darcy backed away from the frigid fury on his face. The muscles beneath her fingers were like iron and she quickly dropped her hand. "I'm sorry. I'm so sorry. He was dreadful."

"Plenty more where he came from."

All she could think was if anyone ever looked at her with eyes that icy, that powerfully cold, she would shatter into tiny shards. "There shouldn't be." She bent down, started to pick up the glass the man had knocked to the floor, but Mac snagged her hand and tugged her up again.

"What are you doing?"

"I was going to clean up the—"

"Stop." His temper was still on the end of a straining leash, and the order snapped out. "You don't belong here," he muttered, and began to pull her away from the tables and the still-gawking crowd. "It isn't all fun and games. It isn't a damn castle. There are people like that in every corner."

"Yes, but—" He was striding so quickly through the breezeway to the hotel area that she had to trot to keep up.

"You ought to be back in Kansas, tucked away in your library."

"I don't want to go back to Kansas."

He pulled her into the elevator and jammed in his master card for her suite. "They'll gobble you up in one tasty bite. I damn near did it myself."

"I don't know what you're talking about."

"Exactly." He rounded on her, frustration, fury, self-disgust punching inside his gut. Her eyes were as big as saucers, that delectably curved top lip just beginning to tremble. "Exactly," he said again, struggling for calm. "I have to go down and take care of this. Stay up here."

"But—"

"Stay up here," he repeated, pausing between each word, then giving her a nudge out of the elevator and into her suite before he did something insane. Like clamping his mouth on hers. "You worry me," he muttered as she stared at him. "You're really starting to worry me."

They continued to stare at each other until the doors shut.

Chapter Four

Darcy kept her spa appointments the next morning because she thought it would be rude not to. But her heart wasn't in it. Even being scrubbed with exotic sea salts, massaged with oils that made her think of some Egyptian handmaiden and having her face packed with thick cool goo the color of ripe pomegranates didn't lift her mood.

He wanted her to leave, and she really had nowhere to go.

It didn't seem to matter that as soon as the documents came through she'd be able to travel to all the dazzling places she'd read and dreamed about. She wanted to stay here, in this wonderful, exciting place, with all the lights and the sounds and the crowds and the seamy edges.

She wanted to gamble again, to drink champagne, to buy more sparkling earrings. She wanted just a little more time in a world where men with faces that should be sculpted in copper paid attention to her as if she were worthy of their interest.

She wanted, more than anything, a few more magical days with Mac before her coach turned into a pumpkin and the glass slipper no longer fit.

She wanted him to smile at her again in the way that transformed his face into one glorious piece of art.

He was so lovely, not just to look at, she thought, but to be with. He had a way of turning those wonderful blue eyes on her and making her think he really cared about what she thought, how she felt, what she had to say.

She'd never been able to talk to another man the way she could talk to him. Without feeling inadequate and foolish. Or simple, she supposed.

But she'd taken up too much of his time, gotten in the way. She'd always been better off fading into a corner and watching other people live. Once you stepped out too far, into those lights, you ended up doing something silly or foolish that made those who knew…*things* wish you'd slip away again.

The money wasn't going to change who she was. A pretty dress, a new haircut—it was only gloss. Under it, she was still awkward and average.

"You're going to love this."

Shaking off the blue mood, Darcy looked over at the technician. She'd already forgotten the woman's name, which was, in Darcy's opinion, as rude as not keeping the appointment in the first place. Flat on her back on the padded table, she focused on the nameplate pinned to the breast of the soft pink uniform.

"Am I, Angie?"

"Absolutely."

To Darcy's shock, Angie tugged down the thin blanket and began to paint warm brown mud on her breasts. "Oh!"

"Too warm?"

"No, no." She would not blush, she would not blush, she would *not* blush. "What's this for?"

"To make your skin irresistible."

"Nobody's going to see it where you're putting it on," Darcy said dryly, and Angie laughed.

"Hey, this is Vegas. Your luck could change any time."

"Maybe you're right." Giving up, Darcy closed her eyes.

She and her new, irresistible skin had barely stepped back into her suite when the buzzer sounded. Her tongue tied itself into knots the minute she opened the door and saw Mac.

"Got a minute?" he asked, then stepped inside when she only nodded. "I don't have much time, but I wanted to let you know the press has the bit between their teeth. The mystery woman angle has them fired up. They'll play that for a few more days, but it won't stop there. There's bound to be a leak sooner rather than later. You'll need to be prepared for that."

"I'm not going back to Kansas." It came out in a burst, fueled by an anger that surprised them both.

Mac raised his eyebrows. "So you said."

"I'm not going back," she repeated. "I have enough of the cash you advanced me to get a hotel room."

"And you'd do that because…"

"You said I shouldn't be here."

"I don't believe I did." But he remembered his temper of the night before, and thought he might have said something along those lines. "It's certainly not what I meant." Annoyed with himself, he dragged a hand through his hair. "Darcy—"

"I know I've been taking up a lot of your time. You feel responsible for me, but you don't have to. I'm perfectly content to keep out of the way. I can just stay up here and write. That's what I did last night after…well, after."

He held up a hand, guessing correctly it would stop the flood of words. "I'm sorry. I was out of line. I let that idiot last night get to me, and I took it out on you." He dipped his hands into his pockets. "But it did make me realize that you shouldn't have been there, and that you certainly shouldn't be wandering around a casino alone."

She'd been on the point of yielding when his final statement put her back up again. "You think I'm stupid and naive."

"I don't think you're stupid."

Her eyes flashed, fascinating him with the sudden and unexpected fire of gold. "Just naive, then. Probably a bit incompetent and certainly too…" Her mind went on a fumbling search for the word. "Too midwestern to take care of myself in the big, bad city."

His eyebrow arched in a way she found both charming and infuriating. "You are the one who walked into town with less than ten dollars, no purse and nothing but the clothes on her back, aren't you?"

"So what! It got me here, didn't it?"

"Point taken," he murmured.

"And last night wasn't the first time I've seen an evil-minded drunk, either. I'm from Kansas, not Dogpatch. We've got plenty of drunks in Kansas."

"I stand corrected." And struggling mightily not to grin.

"And you needn't feel obligated to look after me as if I were some stray puppy who might run out into traffic. There's absolutely no reason for you to worry about me."

"I didn't say I was worried about you. I said you worried me."

"It's the same thing."

"It's entirely different."

"How?"

He studied her. Color was warm in her face, her eyes were dark and shining. It wasn't just anger she was feeling, he realized, but bruised pride as well. And that was undeniably his fault. He sighed. "You're really leaving me no choice. You worry me," he repeated, and laid his hands on her shoulders. "Because…" Slid them down her arms, around her waist. Watched her lips part in surprise just before he covered them with his.

The world tilted. Every coherent thought in her mind tumbled out and scattered. Hopelessly lost. His mouth was just as she'd imagined it would be. Hot and firm and clever. But now it was on hers, luring her into some exciting airless space where everything shimmered and shook.

Colors brightened, blurring around the edges before they melted together and turned as liquid as her bones.

His tongue swept over hers, teasing, inviting, mixing his dark, intimate taste with her own. Smooth, so smooth, that glide of tongue, that slide of lips, that she seemed to coast bonelessly down the long chute of sensation toward a spreading pool of liquid heat.

Her hands had come up to clutch at his arms for balance. He could feel the pressure of her short nails through his jacket, a contrasting signal of anxiety even as her lips opened and gave. Nerves and surrender, a dangerous mix, punctuated by the helpless little whimpers of pleasure that sounded in her throat, combined to take him deeper than he'd intended, to make him want more, much more than he'd expected.

What he'd begun churned through him and demanded he finish—his way. Then and there, and thoroughly. She was aroused. So was he. However innocent, she wasn't a child. And he wanted her. God, he wanted her.

Her eyes remained closed as he drew her away.

He watched the tip of her tongue trace her curvy, unpainted lips before she pressed those lips together, like a woman lingering over a particularly lush taste. Even as her lashes fluttered, a hot fist of need balled in his gut.

Her eyes were dark and clouded, fixed now on his. A flush glowed on her cheeks. A swallow rippled her throat.

Damn, he wanted, desperately wanted to take her in one greedy gulp until nothing was left but the sighs.

"Why…" Her breath was coming too fast for the words to be steady. "Why did you do that?"

Be careful with her, he reminded himself. Very careful. "Because I wanted to. Is that a problem?"

She stared at him for a long moment. "No," she answered with such weighty seriousness he nearly smiled. "I don't think so."

"Good. Because I'm not finished yet."

"Oh." His arms were tightening, easing her close again. Bodies met again. "Well…" Her eyes drifted shut. "Take your time."

Her innocence was as bright as a beacon, and outrageously arousing. No, not a child, he thought again, but the odds were weighted heavily against her. And he had no right to use that as leverage. Grappling for control, he rested his forehead on hers. Slow down, he ordered himself. Better yet, stop.

"Darcy, you're a dangerous woman."

Her eyes flew open. "Me?"

The shock in her voice did nothing to relieve the tension centered in his gut. The tension was a bad sign, he decided, a signal not just of desire, but of desire for her. Very specific, very exact and completely inappropriate. "Lethal," he murmured, then stepped back.

But he kept his hands on her shoulders, not quite able to break all contact. She was searching his face now, her big gold eyes still blurred from the first kiss, her mouth pursed in anticipation of the next. He could have lapped her up like cream.

"Have you ever had a lover?"

She blinked, then her gaze lowered to stare at the buttons of his shirt. The shirt was black and silky. It had felt warm and smooth under her hands. She wanted to touch it again. To touch him. "Not exactly."

His brow lifted again. "Despite its infinite and entertaining varieties, sex remains a fairly exact pastime."

She had the distinct impression he didn't intend to kiss her again after all. Sexual frustration was a new, and not entirely pleasant, sensation. Vaguely insulted, she frowned up at him. "I know what sex is."

No, he thought, she didn't. She didn't have a clue what he wanted to do with her, to her. If she did, he imagined she'd run as far and as fast as her pretty fairy legs would carry her. "You don't know me, Darcy. You don't know the rules around here, or the pitfalls."

"I know how to learn," she said testily. "I'm not a moron."

"Some things you're better off not learning." He gave her shoulders a light squeeze when the phone began to ring. "Answer the phone."

She turned on her heel, stalked over to the desk and snatched up the receiver. "Yes? Hello?"

"And who might this be?"

The abrupt demand in a thick burr was so commanding she answered immediately. "This is Darcy Wallace."

"Wallace? Wallace, is it? And would you spring from William Wallace, the great hero of Scotland?"

"Actually…" Confusion had her pushing a hand through her hair. "He's an ancestor on my father's side."

"Good blood. Strong stock. You can be proud of your heritage, lass. Darcy, is it? And are you a married woman, Darcy Wallace?"

"No, I'm not. I—" She snapped back and her brows drew together. "Excuse me, who is this?"

"This is Daniel MacGregor, and I'm pleased to make your acquaintance."

She managed to close her mouth, take a breath. "How do you do, Mr. MacGregor?"

"I do fine, fine and dandy, Darcy Wallace. I'm told my grandson is paying a call on you."

"Yes, he's here." Weren't her lips still tingling from his? "Um. Would you like to speak to him?"

"That I would. You have a fine, clear voice. How old might you be?"

"I'm twenty-three."

"I wager you're a healthy girl, too."

Totally at sea, she nodded her head. "Yes, I'm healthy." She only blinked at Mac when he cursed under his breath and grabbed the phone away from her.

"Shall I check her teeth for you, Grandpa?"

"There you are." Pleasure, and no remorse, rang in Daniel's voice. "Your secretary transferred me. Of course, I wouldn't have to be transferred all over hell and back to have a word with my oldest grandchild if you ever bothered to call your grandmother. She's feeling neglected."

It was an old ploy, and made Mac sigh. "I called you and Grandma less than a week ago."

"At our age, boy, a week's a lifetime."

"Bull." He couldn't stop the smile. "You'll both live forever."

"That's the plan. So, I hear from your mother—who bothers to call home from time to time—that you lost yourself a million-eight and change."

Mac ran his tongue around his teeth, glancing over as Darcy wandered to the window. "You win some, you lose some."

"True enough. And was the lass I was just speaking to the one who scalped you?"

"Yes."

"A Wallace. Good, clear voice, good manners. Is she pretty?"

Mac eased a hip on the desk. He knew his grandfather well. "Not bad, if you overlook the hunchback and the crossed eyes." Idly he flipped open the notebook on the desk as Daniel's hearty laughter rang in his ear.

"She's pretty then. Got your eye on her, do you?"

Mac lifted his gaze from the pages crowded with margin-to-margin writing, and studied the way Darcy stood facing the window. The sun was a halo over her hair. Her hands were linked together in front of her. She looked as delicate as a wildflower in the unforgiving heat of the desert.

"No." He said it definitely, finally, wanting to mean it. "I don't."

"And why not? Are you going to stay single all your life? A man your age needs a wife. You should be starting a family."

As Daniel blustered on about responsibility, duty, the family name, Mac cocked his head and read a page. It was about a woman sitting alone in the dark, watching the lights of the city outside her window. The sense of solitude, of separation, was wrenching.

Thoughtfully he closed the book again, laying a hand over it as he watched Darcy watch the city. "But I'm having such fun, Grandpa," he said, when Daniel finally paused for breath, "working my way through all the showgirls."

There was a moment's pause, then a roar of laughter. "You always had a mouth on you. I miss you, Robbie."

Daniel was the only one who ever called Mac by his childhood name—and then he used it rarely. Love, Mac thought, was inescapable. "I miss you, too. All of you."

"Well, if you'd tear yourself away from those showgirls, you could come visit your poor old granny."

Obviously Anna MacGregor wasn't within hearing distance. Mac could imagine the punishment she would mete out if she heard her husband call her "poor," "old" or "granny." "Give her my love."

"I will, though she'd prefer you give it to her yourself. Put the lass back on the phone."

"No."

"No respect," Daniel muttered. "I should have taken a strap to you when you were a boy."

"Too late now." Mac grinned. "Behave yourself, Grandpa. I'll talk to you soon."

"See that you do."

Mac stayed where he was after he replaced the receiver. "I'll apologize for The MacGregor's interrogation."

"It's all right." She kept her back to him, stared out at the sun shining on towering buildings. "He sounds formidable."

"Hard shell, soft center."

"Mmm." She hadn't meant to eavesdrop, but how could she have helped hearing Mac's part of the conversation? The love and exasperation in his voice had touched her. And his words had cleared up her confusion.

Showgirls. Of course he would be attracted to the long legs, the beautiful bodies, the exotic faces. He'd only been curious, she supposed. That's why he'd kissed her. But damn him, damn him for stirring up all this need that she'd managed to live very contentedly without until now.

"I seem to have gotten distracted from the point of coming to see you." He waited for her to turn and face him. At a casual glance she appeared perfectly composed. But he couldn't seem to glance at her casually. He was compelled to search, and a search of those eyes revealed bruises and storms. "Now you're angry."

"No, I'm irritated, but I'm not angry. What was the point," she began, then paused significantly. "Of your coming to see me?"

That flair for sarcasm surprised him. The edge of it pricked at him enough to have him pushing off the desk and shoving his hands into his pockets. "The point was the press. I know you're concerned about your name getting out. We're being deluged with calls for the full story. I can hold them off, but it's bound to leak, Darcy. The hotel employs hundreds, and several people already know your name. Sooner rather than later, one of them is going to talk to a reporter."

"I'm sure you're right." She supposed she should be grateful he'd given her something else to worry about. "I'm sure you think I'm a coward, not wanting Gerald to know where I am."

"I think that's your business."

"I am a coward." She said it defiantly, tossing up her chin in a challenging gesture that contrasted with her words. "I'd rather agree than quarrel, rather run that fight. But that's why I'm here, isn't it? Here with you, about to become wealthy. Cowardice works for me."

"He can't hurt you, Darcy."

"Of course he can." Lifting her hands, she gave a weary sigh. "Words hurt. They bruise the heart and scar the soul. I'd rather be slapped than battered with words." Then she shook her head. "Well, whatever happens, happens. How much time do you think I have before my name gets out?"

"A day or two."

"Then I should make the most of it. I appreciate you letting me know. You must be busy. I don't want to keep you."

"Kicking me out?"

She managed a small smile. "We both know you have other things to do. I don't need you to baby-sit."

"All right." He started for the door, then stopped and turned with his hand on the knob. "I wanted to kiss you again." He watched her gaze flick warily to his face. "A little too much for your own good, and maybe for my own."

Her heart stuttered. "Maybe I'm tired of my own good, and willing to gamble."

Something flashed into his eyes that made her shudder. "High stakes, bad odds. Too risky for a novice, Darcy from Kansas. First rule is never bet what you can't afford to lose."

When he closed the door quietly behind him, she let out the breath she'd been holding. "Why do I have to lose?"

She kept to herself the rest of the day, writing furiously in her notebook. The garage that had towed in her car called to tell her it was repaired. On impulse she asked the mechanic if he knew anyone who would buy it. She was finished with it, after all, and with everything else—save her notebooks—that she'd brought with her from Trader's Corners.

When the mechanic offered her a thousand

dollars, she snapped it up without bargaining, and hurried out to sign over the paperwork.

There was a slick little laptop computer sitting on her desk when she returned, with a note telling her that it was hers to use during her stay, courtesy of The Comanche. Thrilled, Darcy stroked it, examined it, experimented with it, then settled down to transcribe her notes onto the screen.

She worked straight through dinner and into the evening until her eyes blurred and her fingers went numb. Hunger rumbled in her stomach. It was tempting to reach for the phone, to order something to be brought to the room. To stay hidden.

Instead she picked up her purse, squared her shoulders. She was going out, she decided. She'd have a meal, some wine if she wanted. Then, by God, she was going to gamble.

The tables were crowded and the air stung with smoke and perfume when she entered the casino. She wanted to watch, to study. Figure the odds, Mac had said. Learn the rules. She intended to do just that. She liked the world here, the hard-edged brightness of it, the thrill of risk.

She wandered through, loitering by a blackjack table long enough to see a man in shirtsleeves with a thin black cigar clamped between his teeth lose five thousand dollars without flinching.

Amazing.

She studied the spin of the wheel, the teasing bounce of the little silver ball at roulette. Saw stacks of chips come and go. Odd or even. Black or red.

Fascinating.

Behind it all was the never-ending beeps and whistles and clinks of the slots. Lights beckoned. Jackpot. She studied the technique of an elderly woman who leaned on a walker and mumbled to the spinning face of a machine. And gave a cheerleader's shout when quarters cascaded into the metal dish.

"Fifty bucks," the woman said, shooting Darcy a steely smile. "About time this sucker paid off."

"Congratulations. It's poker, isn't it?"

"That's right. Been nickel-and-diming me for two hours. But it's heating up now." She gave the machine a friendly thump with her walker, then stabbed the red button again. "Let's go, sweetheart."

It looked like fun, Darcy decided. Simple, uncomplicated, and an excellent place to start. She walked down the line until she came to an unoccupied machine, then slid onto the stool. After reading the instructions, she put a twenty in the slot and watched her credits light. She pushed the button, grinning as her hand was dealt.

In his office, Mac watched her on-screen. He could only shake his head. In the first place, she was playing like a chump, one credit at a time. If she wanted to hit, she needed to play four, a buck a hand. Now she was holding two kings instead of going for the straight flush.

It was pitifully obvious she'd never played poker before in her life.

Well, he'd keep an eye on her, make certain she didn't lose more than a few hundred.

He glanced over at the door when a knock sounded, then his smile spread with delight when his mother poked her head in. "Hello, handsome."

"Hello, gorgeous." He caught her around the waist in a fierce hug and pressed his lips to her soft, burnished gold hair. "I didn't expect you for another day or two."

"We finished up early." She cupped his face in her hands and smiled at him. "And I wanted to see my boy."

"Where's Dad?"

"He'll be right along. He got waylaid in the lobby so I deserted him."

Mac laughed and kissed her again. She was so beautiful, with soft skin, exotic eyes a unique shade of lavender, and strong facial bones that guaranteed grace and beauty for a lifetime. "Serves him right. Come sit down. Let me get you a drink."

"I would love a glass of wine. It's been a long day." With a sigh Serena sat in one of the leather chairs, stretched out long legs that rustled with silk. "I talked to Caine this morning. He tells me he's getting the paperwork finished up for this woman who hit the big machine here. The press is full of Madam X," she added.

With a short laugh, Mac poured a glass of his mother's favored white wine. "I can't think of a title that suits her less."

"Really. What's she like?"

"See for yourself." He gestured to the screen.

"The little blonde in the blue blouse at the poker slot."

Serena shifted, sipping her wine as she studied the monitor. She lifted a brow as Darcy held a pair of eights and tossed away the best part of a flush. "Not much of a player, is she?"

"Green as they come."

Serena's gambler's heart warmed when Darcy pulled another two eights. "Lucky little thing, though. And pretty. Is it true she was dead broke when she walked in here?"

"Just about down to her last dollar."

"Well, good for her." Serena lifted her glass to toast the screen. "I'm looking forward to meeting her. Oh good, someone's going to give her a little help."

"What?" Alerted, Mac looked back at the screen and saw a man slip onto the stool beside her. He saw the quick, flirtatious grin, the easy brush of a hand on Darcy's shoulder. And Darcy's wide-eyed, attentive smile. "Son of a bitch."

Mac was halfway out the door before Serena could leap to her feet. "Mac?"

"I've got to get down there."

"But why—"

As her son dashed off, Serena decided there was only one way to find out why. She set her wine aside and hurried after him.

Chapter Five

People were so nice, so friendly, Darcy thought. And so helpful, she decided as she smiled at the attractive man in the Stetson who'd settled down beside her at the slots.

His name was Jake, and he was from Dallas which, as he said, practically made them neighbors.

"I'm really new at this," she told him confidentially, and his sunshine blue eyes laughed into hers.

"Why I could spot that right off, sugar. Now like I said first off, you want to plug in the maximum credits for each hand, otherwise you don't get yourself a full payoff when you hit."

"Right." Dutifully Darcy pressed the credit button, then punched for the deal. She studied her hand thoughtfully. "I've got two threes, so I hold them."

"Well now, you could." Jake laid a hand over hers before she could press to hold the cards. "But you see, you're after that royal straight flush, right? That's the jackpot. You got yourself the ace, queen and the jack of hearts there. Couple treys aren't going to get you anything. Even a triple's just keeping you in the game."

She nibbled her lip. "I should throw away the threes?"

"If you're going to gamble—" he winked at her "—you should gamble."

"Right." She furrowed her brow and let the threes go. She plucked an ace and a five. "Oh, well, that's no good." Still she remembered what the blackjack dealer had said, and turned to Jake with a smile. "But I lost correctly."

"There you go." She was cute as a brass button, he thought, sweet as a daisy and looked to be just as easy to pick. Charmed, he leaned in a little closer. "Why don't I buy you a drink, and we'll talk poker strategy."

"The lady's unavailable." Mac dropped a proprietary, and none too gentle hand on Darcy's shoulder.

Her head whipped up, her shoulders tensed. "Mac." He had that frigid look in his eyes again, she noted. Not that he spared her a glance. The ice was all for her new friend from Dallas. "Ah, this is Jake. He was showing me how to play the poker machine."

"So I see. The lady's with me."

Jake ran his tongue around his teeth and, after a brief internal debate, decided he wanted to keep those teeth just where they were. "Sorry, pal. Didn't know I was poaching." He rose, tipped his hat to Darcy. "You hold out for that royal straight flush now."

"Thank you." She held out her hand, confused when Jake's eyes shifted to Mac's before he accepted.

"My pleasure." After a short and silent male exchange, Jake swaggered off.

"I'd been doing it wrong," Darcy began. And that was as far as she got.

"Didn't I tell you not to come down here at night alone?" The fact that he was speaking softly didn't lessen the power and fury behind the words. It only added to them.

"That's ridiculous." She wanted badly to cringe, and had to force herself not to. "You can't expect me to sit in my room all night. I was only—"

"This is exactly why. Ten minutes at a machine and you're getting hit on."

"He wasn't hitting on me. He was helping me."

Mac's opinion of that was short and pithy and put some steel back in Darcy's spine.

"Don't swear at me."

"I was swearing in general." He put a hand under her elbow and hauled her to her feet. "The cowboy wasn't going to buy you a drink to be helpful. He was just priming the pump, and believe me, yours is easily primed."

She started to shake, and realized it was just as much from anger as fear. "Well, if he was, and it is, it's my business."

"My place. My business."

She hissed in a breath, tried to jerk free and failed. "Let go of me. I don't have to stay here. If I'd wanted some overbearing male ordering me around, I'd still be in Kansas."

His smile was as thin and sharp as his name. "You're not in Kansas anymore."

"That's both obvious and unoriginal. Now let go of me. I'm leaving. There are plenty of other places where I can gamble and socialize without being harassed by the management."

"You want to gamble?" To her shock and— God help her—excitement, he backed her up against the machine with something close to murder in his eyes. "You want to socialize?"

"Mac?" Deciding she'd seen quite enough, Serena stepped up, a bright, friendly smile in place. "Aren't you going to introduce me?"

He turned his head and stared. He'd completely, totally forgotten about his mother. He saw easily beyond the smile to the command in her eyes. And felt twelve years old again.

"Of course." With a smoothness that blanketed both his straining temper and embarrassment, he shifted his grip on Darcy's arm. "Serena Mac-

Gregor Blade, Darcy Wallace. Darcy, my mother."

"Oh." Not nearly as skilled as Mac, Darcy didn't come close to hiding both her distress and mortification. "Mrs. Blade. How do you do?"

"I'm so happy to meet you. I just got into town and was about to ask Mac about you." Still smiling, she slid an arm around Darcy's shoulders. "Now I can ask you in person. Let's go get a drink. Mac," she added, casting a smug look over her shoulder as she led Darcy away, "we'll be in the Silver Lounge. Tell your father where I am, will you?"

"Oh sure," Mac muttered. "Fine." He resisted, barely, giving the slot a swift kick, and instead dutifully cashed Darcy out.

In a relatively quiet corner of a cocktail lounge gleaming with silver tables and rich black cushions, Darcy ran her fingers up and down the stem of a glass of white wine. She'd taken one sip, to clear her dry throat, but was afraid to take more.

Mac was probably right about one thing, she'd decided. She didn't hold her liquor very well.

"Mrs. Blade, I'm so terribly sorry."

"Really?" Serena relaxed against the cushions and took stock of the young woman facing her. Prettier still up close, she mused, in a delicate, almost ethereal, way. Big innocent eyes, a doll's mouth, nervous hands.

Not the type her son usually looked at twice, she reflected. She knew very well his taste generally ran to the long, lean and, in her opinion, somewhat brittle sort of woman. She also knew him well enough to be sure he rarely, very rarely lost his temper over one.

"Mac did ask me not to come down to the casino alone at night."

Serena arched a brow. "I can't see that he'd have any right to do that."

"No, but…he's been so kind to me."

"I'm glad to hear that."

"What I mean is, he really only asked me that one thing. It's understandable he'd be angry I didn't listen."

"It's understandable he'd be angry because he's used to getting his way." Serena studied Darcy over the rim of her glass. "That's not your problem."

"He feels responsible for me."

It was said in such a miserably depressed tone that Serena had to swallow a chuckle. She had an inkling her son felt a bit more than responsibility. "He's always taken his responsibilities seriously. Again, not your problem. Now, tell me everything." She leaned forward, inviting confidences. "I've gotten it all second hand—either from what Mac told my husband or the papers. I want the whole story, straight from the source."

"I don't know where to start."

"Oh, at the beginning."

"Well." Darcy contemplated her wine, then risked another sip. "It was all because I didn't want to marry Gerald."

"Really?" Delighted, Serena inched closer. "And who is Gerald?"

An hour later, Serena was fascinated, charmed and feeling sentimentally maternal toward Darcy. She'd already decided to extend her quick trip to several days when she covered Darcy's hand with hers. "I think you've been incredibly brave."

"I don't feel brave. No one's ever been as kind

to me as Mac has, and I've made him so angry. Mrs. Blade—"

"I hope you'll call me Serena," she interrupted. "Especially since I'm going to offer you some unsolicited advice."

"I'd appreciate some advice."

"Don't change anything." Now Serena squeezed Darcy's hand. "Mac will deal with it, I promise you. You be exactly what you are, and you enjoy it."

"I'm attracted to him." Darcy winced then scowled down at her empty glass. "I shouldn't have had the wine. I shouldn't have said that. You're his mother."

"Yes, I am, and as such I'd be insulted if you weren't attracted to him. I happen to think he's a very attractive young man."

"Of course. I mean…" She trailed off, her eyes shifting up, then going wide. "Oh." She barely breathed as she stared at the man who stepped up to the table. "You *are* the war chief."

Justin Blade flashed a grin at her, then slid into the booth beside his wife. "You must be Darcy."

"He looks so much like you. I'm sorry. I don't mean to stare."

"The day I mind being stared at by a pretty young woman is the day life stops being worth living."

Justin draped an arm around his wife's shoulders. He was a tall, lean man with black hair streaked with silver as bright as the table and his eyes were green, sharp and deep in a tanned and weathered face. They skimmed over Darcy with both approval and interest.

"Now I know what Mac meant about the fairy wings. Congratulations on your luck, Darcy."

"Thank you. It doesn't seem real yet." She glanced around the glittery lounge. "None of it does."

"Any plans for your new fortune? Other than giving us the chance to win some of it back."

She smiled now, fully. "Oh, he is like you. Actually, I seem to win a little every time I play." She tried to make it sound apologetic, but spoiled it with a chuckle. "But I have put some back— into the shops and salons."

"A woman after my own heart," Serena declared. "We do have wonderful shops here."

"And they genuflect when they see you

coming." Justin's fingers drifted up into his wife's hair and began toying with the strands.

It made Darcy realize she'd never seen her parents touch like that, so casually, so intimately. Not in public or private. And realizing it made her unbearably sad.

"Another round, ladies?" Even as he asked, Justin was signaling for a waitress.

"Not for me. Thank you. I should go up. I thought I'd look for a new car tomorrow."

"Want company?"

Darcy fumbled with her purse as she rose, and smiled hesitantly at Serena. "Yes, if you'd like."

"I'd love it. Just call my room when you decide what time you want to go. Someone will find me."

"All right. It was nice meeting both of you. Good night."

Justin waited until Darcy was out of earshot before lifting an eyebrow at his wife. "What's going on in your head, Serena?"

"All sorts of interesting thoughts." She turned her head so that her lips brushed his.

"Such as?"

"Our firstborn nearly punched a cowboy for having a mild flirtation with our Kansas pixie."

"Another wine for my wife, Carol, and a draft for me," he said to the waitress before shifting to face Serena. "You must be exaggerating. Duncan's the one who likes to trade punches over pretty women, not Mac."

"I'm not exaggerating in the least. Fangs were bared, Blade," she murmured. "And murder was in the air. I believe he's seriously smitten."

"Smitten?" The word made him laugh, then his laughter faded into unexpected anxiety. "Define 'seriously.'"

"Justin." She patted his cheek. "He's nearly thirty. It has to happen sometime."

"She's not his type."

"Exactly." She felt her eyes sting and sniffled. "She's nothing like his type. She's perfect for him." Resolutely she blinked back the tears. "Or I'll find out if she's perfect before long."

"Serena, you sound uncomfortably like your father."

"Don't be absurd." Sentimental tears dried up with the insult. "I have no intention of manipulating or scheming or plotting." She tossed her head. "I'm simply going to…"

"Meddle."

"Discreetly," she finished, and beamed at him. "You are very attractive." She skimmed her fingers through the silver wings of his hair, lingered there. "Why don't we take these drinks upstairs, up to bed, War Chief."

"You're trying to distract me."

"Of course I am." Her smile was slow, seductive and sure. "Is it working?"

He took her hand to pull her to her feet. "It always has." He kissed her fingers. "Always will."

Habitually, Mac slept from about three in the morning to nine, straddling shifts and ending his day after peak hours. Barring trouble, he could safely leave the full responsibility of the casino for that stretch of time to his shift and pit bosses and floor men. Morning hours routinely were dedicated to the massive paperwork the casino demanded—the banking, accounting, staff meetings, the hirings and firings.

He'd taken over as casino manager of

Comanche Vegas when he'd been twenty-four, and had set the tone. The surface was friendly, noisy, full of movement and action. But underneath, it was ruthlessly organized and the bottom line was profit.

As he was one himself, he could spot a card counter across the blackjack pit after a five-minute study. He knew when to let them ride, or when to move them along. Employees were expected to be personable and honest. Those who met his standards were rewarded. Those who didn't were fired.

There were no second chances.

His father had built The Comanche out of guts and grit, and had turned it into a polished, sharp-edged jewel in the desert. Mac's responsibility was to keep the sheen high and he took his responsibilities seriously.

"The first half of the year looks good." Justin leaned back in his chair, removed the reading glasses he privately despised, then handed Mac back the computer-generated spreadsheet. "Up about five percent from last year."

"Six," Mac said with a flash of grin. "And a quarter."

"You've got your mother's head for math."

"I live for numbers. Where is Mom? I thought she'd want to sit in on this meeting."

"She's off with Darcy."

Mac set down the personnel file he'd just picked up. "With Darcy."

"Shopping. Refreshing young woman." Justin's face was as bland as it would have been if he'd held three aces. "Makes it hard to regret handing her seven figures."

"Yeah." Mac caught himself drumming his fingers on the file and stopped. "The press is pushing for a name. I've got half a dozen assistants fielding calls."

"Even without her name, the publicity's humming. It can't hurt business."

"The hotel manager reports an upswing in reservations in the last two days. Play on the machine she hit on is up thirty percent."

"When her story gets out—and that pretty face is splashed over the national news—they'll flood in here."

"I'm putting on three extra floor men, and I'd like to promote Janice Hawber to pit boss."

"You know your staff." Justin took out a slim cigar. "We'll likely get the ripple effect at other locations." When Mac opened the file, Justin waved the cigar, spiraling smoke. "Let's take a break here. Whatever happened to that long-legged brunette who liked baccarat and Brandy Alexanders?"

"Pamela." His father didn't miss a trick, Mac thought. "I believe she's playing baccarat and drinking Brandy Alexanders over at the Mirage these days."

"Too bad. She added a nice…shine to the tables."

"She was looking for a rich husband. I decided to fold before things got sticky."

"Hmm. Seeing anyone else?" At Mac's lifted brow, Justin grinned. "Just trying to keep up with the tour, pal. Duncan changes dancing partners so often I just give them numbers."

"Duncan juggles women like apples," Mac said, thinking of his brother. "I find one at a time's less complicated. And no, I'm not dancing at the moment. You can report back to Grandpa that his oldest grandchild continues to be lax in his duty to continue the line."

Justin chuckled and puffed on his cigar. "You'd think four great-grandchildren would satisfy him for a while."

"Nothing will satisfy The MacGregor until every last one of us is married and clucking around a brood of kids." Mac moved his shoulders restlessly. "At least he could nag one of the others for a bit. Pick on D.C."

"He does pick on D.C." Justin grinned. "Alan tells me he picks at the boy until D.C. holes up in his garret, paints and swears he'll die a bachelor just to spite Daniel. So then Daniel goes to work on Ian who just smiles charmingly, agrees with everything Daniel says, and cheerfully ignores him."

"Maybe I'll slip one of their names into our next conversation—strictly in the spirit of self-preservation—and shift his focus for a while."

The door burst open. "Speak of the devil," Mac murmured as he got to his feet.

The MacGregor stood in the doorway, grinning widely. His white hair flowed back from a broad and deeply seamed face offset by eyes that twinkled bright blue and a wild, snowy beard. His shoulders were as broad as the grill of a truck. And the hand that slapped Justin enthusiastically on the back was as big as a ham.

"Give me one of those pitiful excuses for a cigar," Daniel boomed, then caught Mac in a bear hug that could have toppled a rabid grizzly. "Pour me a Scotch, boy. Flying cross-country puts a thirst in a man."

"You had a Scotch on the plane." Caine Mac-Gregor strode into the room. "Charmed the flight attendant out of one when I wasn't looking. If Mom finds out, she'll scalp me."

"What she doesn't know won't hurt you." Daniel plopped his bulk into a chair, sighed lustily and looked around with great pleasure. "Well now, how about that cigar?"

Knowing the rules—and Anna MacGregor's wrath—Justin turned to his brother-in-law. "Anna dump him on you?"

"Ha!" Daniel thumped the cane he used as much for looks as for convenience.

"He wouldn't stay home. She sends her love and her sympathy. Good to see you." Caine gave both Justin and Mac a hard hug. "Where's Rena?"

"Shopping," Justin told him. "She should be back shortly."

"Give me a damn cigar." Daniel glowered and thumped his cane again. "And where's the lassie who skinned you for over a million? I want to meet her."

Mac turned to study his grandfather. Formidable, Darcy had said. It appeared she was going to find out firsthand just how formidable.

Dazed and flushed, Darcy carted bags and boxes into her suite. Similarly burdened, Serena was right behind her.

"Oh, that was fun." With a sigh, Serena dumped everything on the floor and dropped into a chair. "My feet are killing me. Always a good sign of shopping success."

"I don't even remember what I bought. I don't know what came over me."

"I'm a terrible influence."

"You were wonderful." It had been one of the most monumental days in Darcy's life. Being propelled from store to store, having blouses and dresses tossed at her, modeling them in front of

Serena's assessing eyes. "You know everything about clothes."

"A lifetime love affair. Darcy, run up and put on that yellow sundress. I'm dying to see it on you again. Try it with the white sandals and the little gold hoop earrings." She rose to nudge Darcy toward the stairs. "Indulge me, won't you, honey? I'll order us up a well-deserved cold drink."

"All right." Halfway up, she turned and looked back. "I had the best time. I don't think I'll be able to bring myself to buy that sports car, though. It's so impractical."

"We'll worry about that later." Humming to herself, Serena walked away to order some lemonade.

The child was starved for attention, she thought. It was so easy to see, and so easy to read between the lines when Darcy spoke of her childhood. She doubted anyone had ever taken her on a whirlwind shopping spree, or giggled with her over foolish lingerie, or told her how pretty she looked in a yellow dress.

It made Serena's heart ache to remember how stunned Darcy had looked when she'd laughed and hugged her as they'd debated over earrings. And the wistful glance she'd sent the bright blue sports car before she'd given her attention to the sober and practical sedan she said was more suitable.

As far as Serena could tell there had been far too much suitable in Darcy's young life, and not nearly enough fun.

That, she determined, was going to change.

When the phone rang, Darcy called from upstairs. "Oh, can you—I'm not—"

"I'll get it." Serena picked up the phone. "Ms. Wallace's suite." Her eyes gleamed, her smile spread as she listened to the voice. "Yes, indeed, we're back."

Her mind calculated at a speed and in a direction that would have made Daniel puff out with pride. "Why don't we do that here? I'm sure she'd be more comfortable. Yes, now's fine. See you in a minute."

Humming again, Serena strolled to the base of the stairs. "Need any help?"

"No. There are so many boxes. I just found the dress."

"Take your time. That was Justin on the phone. You don't mind if we do a little business, do you?"

"No."

"Good. I'll order up more drinks." Champagne, she decided, considering.

Ten minutes later, Darcy took the first turn on the steps just as the elevator opened. She froze where she was, staggered by the rich mix of male voices, the sudden rush of energy that poured out of the elevator along with them.

Then she could only see Mac.

Serena watched the way her son's eyes locked on Darcy's, the way they darkened, held. And she was sure.

"There's my girl." Daniel grabbed his daughter in a fierce hug. "You don't call your mother enough," he scolded her. "She pines."

"I've been spending a lot of time nagging my children." She kissed him lavishly on both cheeks, then turned to embrace her brother. "How are you? How's Diana? How're the kids?"

"Everyone's fine. Diana's tying up a case and couldn't get away. She'll be sorry she missed you."

"Well now." Daniel leaned on his cane and

studied the woman who'd frozen like a statue on the stairs. "You're just a wee lass, aren't you? Come on down, and let's have a better look at you."

"He rarely bites." Mac crossed to the base of the steps, held out a hand.

Her legs were wobbly, and she knew her fingers weren't steady so she pretended not to see his hand. But he took hers anyway, giving it a reassuring squeeze that clutched at her heart.

"Darcy Wallace, The MacGregor."

She was afraid she wouldn't find her voice. He looked so big, and so fierce with white brows knitted together over sharp blue eyes. "I'm happy to meet you, Mr. MacGregor."

The scowl stayed in place another moment, then transformed into a smile so wide and so bright she blinked. "Pretty as a sunbeam." He gave her cheek a gentle pat with his huge hand. "Tiny as an elf."

Her lips curved up in response. "It's only that you're so big. If William of Scotland had had more like you, he would have won."

Daniel let out his bark of a laugh, and winked at her. "Now, there's a lass. Come sit and talk to me."

"You can interrogate her later. I'm Caine MacGregor."

She shifted her gaze to the tall man with silver and gold hair and strong blue eyes. "Yes, I know. I'm so nervous." She clutched her hands together. How many legends could one person meet in one day? "I studied about you in school. Everyone thought you'd run for president."

"I leave the politics to Alan. I'm just a lawyer. Your lawyer," he added, taking her arm and leading her to a chair at the glossy conference table. "Want me to clear this rabble out while we consult?"

"Oh, no, please." She scanned the faces around her, lingered on Mac's. "Everyone here has a part in this."

"All right. It's straightforward enough." He sat and opened his briefcase. "I've got your birth certificate, your social security card, a copy of the police report from the purse snatching last week. You're unlikely to recover anything from that."

She stared down at the papers he handed her. "It doesn't matter. You got all of this so quickly."

"Connections," he said with a wolfish grin. "I

have copies of your last two years' tax returns. There are some forms for you to fill out and sign. A number of them."

"All right." She tried not to gape at the stack he began to produce. "Where do I start?"

"I'll explain them as we go along." He glanced up, wiggling his brows at his family. "Haven't you all got something better to do?"

"No." Daniel took a chair for himself. "Can't a man get a drink around here while all this legal mumbo jumbo's going on?"

"I ordered drinks." To distract him, Serena sat on the arm of his chair and began to tell him about her grandchild's latest accomplishments.

Listening carefully, Darcy filled out each form. She hesitated over the address, then wrote in the name of the hotel. When Caine didn't correct her, she relaxed a little and continued to note down the required information.

"Your identification's in order," Caine told her. "You'll be able to reapply for a driver's license, credit cards, that sort of thing. You didn't indicate a bank."

"A bank?"

"The transfer of funds will be done electronically, from account to account. The oversize check Mac will present you with is just for publicity. Photo op, and positive publicity for The Comanche. The actual business is accomplished quickly and efficiently by transferring the amount of your winnings from The Comanche's account to yours. Do you want the money sent to your bank in Kansas?"

"No." She refused swiftly, then fell into silence.

"Where do you want it sent, Darcy?" Caine asked gently.

"I don't know. Maybe it could just stay in the same bank. Here?"

"That's not a problem. You're aware that the IRS gets the first bite."

She nodded, signing her name to the last form. Under her lashes, she watched Mac go to the door to let in the room-service waiter.

Mac wore black trousers and a white shirt. Both looked soft, almost fluid, and she wondered about the texture, wished she could run her fingertips over them. Over him.

"You're going to need financial advice."

"What?" Flushing, berating herself for not paying attention, she looked over at Caine. "I'm sorry."

"Tomorrow morning, you're going to have a great deal of money. You'll need a financial advisor."

"You can't do that?"

"I can give you some basic and initial guidance. After that, you're going to want someone who specializes. I can give you some names."

"I'd appreciate it."

"That's pretty much it." He leaned back. "We'll open you an account, the money will be transferred. And you're set."

"Just like that?"

"Just like that."

"Oh." She pressed a hand to her suddenly jittery stomach. "God." Once again she searched out Mac's face, hoping he'd tell her what to do, what to say. But he only watched her, his eyes steady and unreadable.

With an impatient huff for her son, Serena

rose. "I'd say this calls for a celebration. Mac, darling, open the champagne. Darcy, you get the first glass."

"It's so nice of you, all of you, but—" She jolted when the cork popped.

"I've never lost a million to anyone more appealing." Justin took the glass from his son and carried it to Darcy. "Enjoy it." He leaned down to kiss her cheek.

Warmth spread in her stomach, pressure weighed on her chest. "Thank you."

"Congratulations." Caine took her hand, covered it with both of his.

Then everyone was lifting glasses, and talking. She was hugged, kissed by everyone, with the notable exception of Mac. He only lifted a hand to her cheek, skimmed a finger down it.

There was laughing, and arguments over the time and place for a family dinner, which, she realized with shock, included her. Serena draped an arm casually around her shoulder while telling Caine he was an idiot if he thought she'd settle for pizza for such an occasion.

Emotions were clawing at her, rising up to

squeeze her heart, to close her throat and burn her eyes. She heard her own breath begin to hitch and clamped down hard.

"Excuse me." She managed to mumble it before turning quickly for the stairs. Horribly aware the laughter had stopped, she rushed up, closed herself in the bathroom. She held on, carefully turning the water on full in the sink so the sound would cover her sobs.

She sat on the floor, curled up into herself and wept like a baby.

Chapter Six

The suite was quiet when Darcy came out again. She didn't know whether to be relieved or mortified to realize they'd left her alone. She would have to fumble her way through apologies and explanations, she told herself. But for now she could settle her nerves and emotions.

She glanced around the bedroom, scanning the shopping bags, the boxes. The right thing to do, she told herself, was to put everything away, to tidy up, to put at least this part of her life in order.

She was just unwrapping a new blouse when

she heard footsteps on the stairs. Clutching the blouse, she stared at Mac as he stopped at the top of the suite.

"Are you all right?"

"Yes. I thought everyone had gone."

"I stayed," he said simply, then crossed to her. He glanced down at the blouse she continued to hold in white-knuckled fingers. "Nice color."

"Oh. Yes. Your mother picked it out." Feeling foolish, Darcy relaxed her fingers and turned away to hang the blouse in the closet. "I was so rude, leaving that way. I'll apologize to everyone."

"There's no need for that."

"Of course there is." She spent several seconds adjusting the shoulders of the blouse on the padded hanger as if their evenness was of monumental importance. "It's just that everything seemed to hit me all at once." She went back to unfold slacks, then repeated the procedure, lining up the edges of the hem perfectly.

"That's understandable, Darcy. It's a lot of money. It'll change your life."

"The money?" Distracted, she glanced back,

then fluttered her hands. "Well, yes, I suppose the money's part of it."

He angled his head. "What else?"

She started to pick up a box, then set it back on the bed and wandered to the window. It still felt odd to stand there against the glass, with a world she'd only begun to touch spread like a banquet at her feet.

"Your family's so…beautiful. You have no idea what you have. You couldn't. They've always been yours, you see, so how could you know."

She watched the signs of the casino across the street, beckoning, daring, inviting. *Win, Win, Win.*

It wasn't so terribly hard to win, she thought. But it was much, much trickier to keep the prize.

"I'm a watcher," she told him. "I'm good at it. That's why I want to write. I want to write about things I see, or want to see. Things I'd like to feel or experience." She lifted her hands to rub her arms, then made herself turn back to him. "I watched your family."

She looked so lovely, he thought. And so lost. "And what did you see?"

"Your father playing with your mother's hair

when they sat together in the lounge last night."
She saw the confusion in his eyes and smiled.
"You're used to seeing them touch each other—
casually, affectionately, so you don't notice when
it happens. Why would you?" she murmured,
swamped with envy. "He put his arm around her,
and she leaned into him, sort of…" Eyes half-
closed, she moved her body as if yearning for
another. "Settled into the curve because she knew
exactly how she'd fit there."

Darcy closed her eyes, laid a hand over her
own heart as she brought the scene back into
focus. "And while he talked to me, he toyed
with the ends of her hair. Tangled them,
combed them through, wound the strands
around his finger. It was lovely. She knew he
was doing it, because there was a little light in
her eyes. I wonder if it takes another woman to
recognize that."

She opened her eyes again and smiled. "I never
saw my parents touch that way. I think they loved
each other, but they never touched that way, that
easy and wonderful way. Some people don't. Or
they can't."

She sighed and shook her head. "I'm not making sense."

He could see it himself, now that she'd painted it for him. And she was right, he realized. It was so much a part of his life, a part of his family, he didn't notice it.

"Yes, you are."

"It's more—it's all of it. Everyone piling in here a little while ago. You were part of it again, so you couldn't have really seen it. The way your grandfather hugged your mother. So strong and tight. For that instant she was the center of his world, and he of hers. And more, when she sat on the arm of his chair. He laid his hand on her knee. Just put it there, to touch. It was so lovely," she said quietly. "The way she and your uncle argued about where to have dinner, and laughed at each other. All the little looks and pats and the shorthand of people who know each other, and like each other."

"They do like each other." He could see that her eyes were overbright again, and reached out to touch her hair. "What is it, Darcy?"

"They were so kind to me. I'm taking money

from them, a lot of money, but everyone's drinking champagne and laughing and congratulating me. Your mother put her arm around my shoulders." It made her voice break, forced her to fight to steady it. "It sounds ridiculous, I know it, but if I hadn't gone up right then, I would have grabbed onto her. Just grabbed on and held. She would have thought I was crazy."

Lonely? Had he thought she was lonely? He understood now the word didn't come close. "She would have thought you wanted a hug." He slipped his arms around her, felt her tremble lightly. "Go ahead, grab onto me. It's all right."

He eased her closer, pressed his cheek to her hair. He could feel her hesitation, the battle of emotions that had her standing very still. Then her arms came around him, wrapped tight. Her breath came out on a long, broken sigh.

"We're big on grabbing in my family," he told her. "You won't shock any of us if you take hold."

It felt so good to press up against the strong wall of his chest, to hear the steady beat of his heart, to smell the warmth of his skin. Closing her eyes, she let herself absorb the comfort of his hand stroking gently over her back.

"It's just so foreign to me. All of this. All of them. You. Especially you."

Her voice was husky and low. Her hair was soft under his cheek and fragrant as a meadow. Affection, he reminded himself as her slender little body molded to his, not lust. Friendship, not passion.

Then she turned her head as if to sniff his neck and needs stirred restlessly.

"Better now?" He started to ease away, but she clung. His lips brushed her temple, lingered. He held her, let her hold him and told himself it was only because she needed it.

"Mmm."

The dress had thin straps crossing over the smooth flesh of her back. His fingers began to trace along them, under them. She moved in a long, catlike stretch under the caress, jangling his brain.

It was the only excuse he had for the fact that his lips trailed down her face, found hers and plundered.

He forgot to be gentle. She was pressed against

him in the stream of sunlight, all gold and soft and willing. The kiss demanded surrender, and she gave it, flowing into his arms like heated wine, her mouth yielding under the assault of his as if it had only been waiting. Had always been waiting.

Her mind was spinning in slow, expanding circles that spiraled up toward something desperately wanted. The strength of him, the power of those arms that wrapped possessively around her was desperately exciting. Knowing she was helpless against him made her quiver, yet she gloried in the power of him.

This was need, she thought wildly. This, finally this. A wild burst of light and energy and raw nerves. The thumping heart, the racing pulse, the explosion of heat.

Thrilled, she gave herself to it, to him.

In one strong stroke, his hands slid down her back, over the curve of her bottom, lifting her, pressing heat desperately to heat. His mouth swallowed her gasps, greedily, ravenously. He could imagine himself filling her, buried in her, taking her where they stood and driving into her until the hot ball of frustration broke free and gave him peace.

He caught himself as his hands gripped those delicate straps over her back, at the point of rending. He looked down into her eyes, wide, unseeing and still swollen from tears.

He set her aside so abruptly she staggered, scalded her with a look when she crossed her hands over her heart as if to hold it in place.

"You're too damn trusting." The words whipped out at her, but the lash was for himself. "It's a miracle you survived a day on your own."

God, my God, was all she could think. Was the blood supposed to burn like this? It was a wonder her skin didn't burst into flame. She lifted her fingers to her mouth where her lips continued to tingle and ache. "I know you won't hurt me."

He'd come close, dangerously close, to ripping off her clothes, shoving her against the wall and taking her without thought or care. Now, he thought, she was standing there, staring at him out of eyes filled with arousal and—worse, much worse—trust.

"The hell I won't." He said it roughly, hoping

to save them both. "You don't know me, and you don't know the game, so I'll tell you, don't bet against the house. The house always wins in the end. Always."

She couldn't catch her breath. "I won."

His eyes flashed. "Stick around," he challenged. "I'll get it back. And more. More than you'll want to lose. So be smart."

His hand whipped out, cupped the back of her neck firmly. He wanted her to cringe. If she did he'd be able to resist all the things he wanted to do. "Run away. Take the money and run far and fast. Buy yourself a house with a picket fence and a hatchback in the driveway and shade trees in the yard. Because my world isn't yours."

She almost shuddered at his words. But if she did, she'd prove everything he said was true. "I like it here."

His lips curved into something between a smile and a sneer. "Honey, you don't even know where you are."

"I'm with you." And that, she realized with a fresh and towering thrill, was all she really wanted.

"You think you want to play with me?" He angled his hand at the back of her neck to bring her to her toes. "Little Darcy from Kansas? First raise and you'll fold your cards and scramble."

"You don't scare me."

"Don't I?" He damn well should, he thought. And he damn well would, for her own good. "You haven't even got the guts to risk having some jerk back home find out where you are. You'd rather sneak out of your own town like a thief instead of taking a stand. Now you think you can play with the high rollers?" With another short laugh, he released her and turned to leave. "Not bloody likely."

His words were a sharp slap of shame to an exposed cheek. She winced from the blow but steadied herself. "You're right."

He stopped at the top of the stairs and turned back. She was still standing by the window with her arms wrapped tight around her body, her eyes lit with a passion that contrasted sharply with the defensive stance.

He wanted, quite desperately, to go back,

gather her close again and just hold. Not simply because she needed it, he realized with something kin to panic. Because he did. Outrageously.

Her breath came out in one explosive puff. "You're absolutely right. How do we do it?"

The images that careered through his mind had him taking careful hold of the banister. "Excuse me?"

"How do we inform the press? Do you just give out my name, or do we have to do something like a release or a press conference?"

The combination of shame and irritation he felt was lethal. He took a moment, rubbing a hand over his face as he searched for control. "Darcy, there's no point in rushing into that."

"Why wait?" She stiffened her spine. "You said that it was going to leak shortly anyway. I'd prefer to have some control. And I can hardly expect you to have any respect for me if I continue to hide this way."

"This isn't about me. It's long past time you started thinking not just *for* yourself, but thinking *of* yourself."

"I am. And it is about me." Odd, she thought,

how saying that, realizing that, felt so calming. "It's about taking a stand, not being pushed around, pressured or maneuvered. I might not be a high roller, Mac, but I'm ready to play my hand."

She turned, moving quickly before she could change her mind, and picked up the bedside phone. "Do you call the press, or do I?"

He studied her another moment, waiting for her to fold. But her eyes stayed level, her jaw remained set. Saying nothing, he walked to her, took the phone out of her hand, then punched in an extension.

"This is Blade. I need you to set up a press conference. We'll use the Nevada Suite. One hour."

"I pushed her into this." Behind the service entrance of the Nevada Suite, Mac shoved his hands into his pockets and watched as Caine briefed Darcy on the press conference.

"You gave her breathing room," Serena corrected. "If you hadn't run interference, she'd have been dropped straight into the media days ago. Without time to settle and prepare." She gave her son a quick, supportive pat on the arm. "And without one of the top lawyers in the country beside her."

"She's not ready for this."

"I think you underestimate her."

"You didn't see her an hour ago."

"No." And though she wondered what had passed between Darcy and her son, she resisted prying. "But I'm seeing her now. And I say she's ready."

Serena linked an arm through her son's and studied the woman listening attentively to Caine. Darcy had topped the yellow sundress with a short white jacket. It was a smart look, Serena decided. Simple and sunny.

The girl was a little pale, she mused, but she was holding her own.

"She's going to surprise herself," Serena murmured. And you, she added silently. "Caine's going to be right there with her—and all of us are here, backing her up."

Justin slipped through the heavy door, nodded to his son, laid a hand lightly on his wife's shoulder. "We're set. The natives are a bit restless. Do you want me to make the announcement?"

"I'll do it." He watched the way his mother's hand lifted to lie over his father's, the way their bodies brushed. The unit they made. It was something so natural to both of them, he realized he wouldn't have noticed, or would have taken it for granted. Until Darcy.

"I haven't appreciated you enough." He covered their joined hands with his. "Not nearly enough."

Justin frowned thoughtfully as Mac walked to Darcy. "Now, what was that about?"

"I'm not sure." Serena smiled, a bit mistily. "But I like it. Let's go keep The MacGregor distracted so Darcy can get through this smoothly."

Darcy was terrified. Everything Caine had told her was already jumbled into mush in her head. Pride kept her rooted to the spot even when her imagination conjured a picture of herself running like a rabbit.

Her heart drummed hard staccato beats in her head as Mac came toward her.

"Ready?"

Time to stop running, she told herself. "Yes."

"I'm going to go in, give them a brief rundown,

then you'll come in and field some questions. That's all there is to it."

He might as well have told her she was to perform a tap dance while juggling swords. But she nodded. "Your uncle's explained how it works."

"The girl's not a moron," Daniel barked. "She knows how to speak for herself. Don't you, lass?"

The bright blue eyes demanded confidence. "We're about to find out." She squared her shoulders and walked to the side door to peek out. "So many." Her stomach did a painful lurch as she scanned the dozens of faces in the ballroom. "Well." She stepped back. "One or a hundred it's the same thing."

"Don't answer anything you're not comfortable with," Mac said briefly, then stepped out.

The noise level rose with rustling movements and speculative murmurs as he climbed the short stairs to a long platform.

Confidence, Darcy reflected, watching the way he moved, the easy way he stood behind the dais and spoke into the microphone. His voice was clear, his smile easy. When laughter broke out among the gathered reporters, she blinked.

She hadn't heard the words, just the tone. She understood he was setting a casual and friendly one.

It was so easy for him, she thought. Facing strangers, thinking on his feet, being in control. The sea of faces didn't have his nerves jangling, the shouted questions didn't shake his poise in the least.

"Okay?" Caine put a hand to the small of her back.

She drew in a breath, held it, let it out. "Okay."

Attention shifted in a wave when she stepped out. Cameras whirled as photographers jockeyed for a better angle. Television crews zoomed in. A barrage of questions was hurled at her the minute she stepped up to the mike. She jolted a little when Mac reached down to adjust it for her.

"I—" Her voice boomed back at her, making her want to giggle nervously. "I'm Darcy Wallace. I, ah…" She cleared her throat and struggled to dredge something coherent out of the jumble of thoughts in her mind. "I hit the jackpot."

There was laughter, some appreciative applause. And the questions shot out too fast to separate one from the other.

"Where are you from?"

"How do you feel?"

"What are you doing in Vegas?"

"What happened when…"

Why? How? Where?

"I'm sorry." Her voice frayed around the edges, but when Mac moved closer, she shook her head fiercely. She would do this, she promised herself. And she would do it without making a fool of herself. "I'm sorry," she repeated. "I've never talked to reporters before, so I don't really know how. Maybe it would be better if I just told you what happened."

It was easier that way, like telling a story. As she spoke, her voice steadied, and the fingers that had gripped the edges of the dais like a lifeline relaxed.

"What was the first thing you did when you realized you'd won?"

"After I fainted?" There was such quick laughter at her answer that her lips curved up in a smile. "Mr. Blade gave me a room—a suite. They have beautiful rooms here, like something out of a book. There's a fireplace, and a piano and gorgeous flowers. I don't think it all even started to sink in until the next day. Then the first thing I did was buy a new dress."

"Lass has a way with her," Daniel announced.

"She's caught them." Serena beamed approval. "She has no idea how charming she is."

"Our boy's taken with her." Daniel wiggled his eyebrows when his daughter sent him an arched look. "See how he hovers over her, like he's ready to scoop her up and cart her off if anyone gets too close. He's smitten."

She wasn't quite ready to give him the satisfaction of agreeing. "They've only known each other a few days."

Daniel merely snorted, then leaned in close to whisper in her ear. "And how long did it take you to catch this one's eye?" He jerked a shoulder toward Justin.

"Slightly less time than it took me to realize you'd maneuvered us together in the first place."

"Married thirty years now, aren't you?" Unrepentant, Daniel grinned. "No, don't thank me," he continued, patting her cheek. "A man's got to look after his family, after all. They'll make pretty babies together, don't you think, Rena?"

She only sighed. "At least try to be subtle about it."

"Subtle's my middle name," Daniel said with a wink.

"Good job." Caine gave Darcy a congratulatory embrace the minute the door closed behind them.

"It wasn't as hard as I thought it would be." Relief flooded through her. "And now it's over."

"It's just beginning," Caine corrected, sorry to put that doe-on-alert look back in her eyes. "Mac will keep them busy for now," he said, nodding as his nephew went out to bat cleanup for the press.

"But I told them everything."

"They're always going to want more. And you can expect dozens of calls requesting personal interviews, photos. Offers for your life story."

"My life story." That, at least, made her laugh. "I barely had a life before a few days ago."

"The contrast is only going to add fuel. The

tabloids are going to play with this, so be prepared for speculation that you were directed to Vegas by psychic aliens."

When she laughed, he guided her at a quick pace toward the service elevator. He didn't want to frighten her, or dull that bloom of success, but knew she needed to be prepared.

"The calls to offer you tremendous investment opportunities are going to start, too. Financial advisors, legitimate and not, are going to camp on your doorstep. The stepsister of the cousin of the kid who sat behind you in first grade is going to try to hit you up for a loan."

"That would be Patty Anderson," Darcy improvised with a weak smile. "I never liked her anyway."

"Good girl. Do yourself a favor. Don't answer the phone for a couple of days. Better yet, we can arrange for Mac to have the desk take your calls until things cool off a bit."

"That's like running again, isn't it?"

"No. It's protecting yourself, and it's staying in control. If you want to do interviews, you can set them up. When you've figured out what it is you want to do, you contact a financial advisor. Whatever you do, you do at your pace."

"I'm in charge," Darcy said when they stopped at the door of her suite.

"Exactly. If you have any questions or concerns, you can call me. I'll be around through tomorrow. After that, you can reach me in Boston."

"I don't know how to begin to thank you."

"Enjoy yourself." He gave the hand she offered a squeeze. "And don't forget how much fun it was to buy a new dress."

"Keep it simple," she murmured, understanding.

"Atta girl." He bent to kiss her cheek. "I'll see you later."

Alone, Darcy stepped into the suite. Keeping it simple wasn't as easy as it sounded. She was a rich woman with her fifteen minutes of fame in its initial seconds. The message light on her phone was blinking, and the phone itself began to ring. Taking Caine's advice, she ignored it, waiting until it stopped, then taking the receiver off the hook.

Problem solved, she thought, for now.

But she had much deeper, much more complex problems that sudden wealth had nothing to do with.

She was in love and knew there was no point in questioning it, debating it or denying it. Her heart was the one thing she'd always been sure of.

Often she'd imagined what it would be like to lose it, the thrill and the anxiety of the fall. She'd always wondered who it would be who would make everything inside her yearn. How they would be together—for in her dreams he'd loved her as well.

But this wasn't a dream or imagination. Loving Mac was simply and brutally real, with the physical needs so much sharper and more vital than she'd believed herself capable of.

She wanted him, to touch him, to taste, to fulfill the promise of that frantic kiss. She wanted to tremble with the knowledge she was desirable, and oh, she wanted to know what it was to lose herself in sensations.

Just as much, she wanted to curl up against him and know she was welcome there. Even expected there. She wanted to exchange those quiet looks that people who were truly intimate could use as effectively as words.

To be loved in return.

That wasn't a simple matter.

But something about her stirred him, and that in itself was a miracle. If he could want her, perhaps there was a chance for more. It wasn't any more impossible, she supposed, than winning more than a million dollars on the single pull of a lever.

Comforted by that, she snuggled into the corner of the sofa, rested her head on the big, soft pillow tucked there and let herself imagine.

She dreamed of showgirls, dozens of them with endless legs and bountiful breasts showcased in brief, glittering costumes and colorful, floating feathers.

She stood among them, miles too short, wearing layers too plain to be noticed. A wren among exotic birds.

Their long legs flashed, their lush bodies turned and twirled while she stumbled through the complex routine. She couldn't keep up, couldn't compete. No matter how hard she tried, she was always a step behind.

Mac stood watching, a small, amused smile on his face. Beautiful women with long, curvy bodies spun gracefully, seductively around him. Take your pick, they seemed to say.

His gaze flicked down to her face when she stopped in front of him. *Where did you come from? You don't belong here.*

But I want to stay.

He only patted her cheek, then gently nudged her along. *This isn't the place for you, Darcy from Kansas. You don't even know where you are.*

I do know. I do. And it could be the place for me. I want it to be.

And there was Gerald, taking her hand, tugging her away. He had that impatient frown on his face, that irritated scowl in his eyes.

It's time to stop this foolishness. If you insist on pretending to be what you're not, you're only going to embarrass yourself. I'm tired of waiting for you to come to your senses. We're going home.

"I'm not going back." She murmured it as she broke through the surface of the dream. "I'm not going back," she said more definitely, opening her eyes to find the room had become dark while she'd slept.

She lay there another moment, ordering both the dream and the depression that accompanied it to fade.

"I'm staying here." She wrapped her arms around the pillow. "No matter what."

Chapter Seven

Darcy had been at The Comanche nearly a week and was amazed at how much of the hotel she'd yet to explore.

She'd managed to catch the stunning display of horsemanship presented in the auditorium twice a day, where beautiful fast horses and daring riders in authentic Comanche costumes teamed up for a spectacular performance.

She'd wandered around the lavish outdoor pool with its sparkling water contained in bright tile cannily shaped in a wide *C,* and dipped her fingers into the smaller lagoon, secluded by palms and fed by a musical waterfall.

She'd indulged herself in the spa and treatment center, had roamed nearly half the wide array of shops, but had yet to slip inside any of the three theaters or walk through the many ballrooms and conference rooms, or find an excuse to visit the business center.

The longer she was a guest of The Comanche, she thought, the more it seemed to grow.

When the elevator let her out on the roof, she stepped into a lush oasis of palms and tangling flowered vines. The morning sun showered onto the rich blue waters of the pool, shooting diamonds of light onto the surface.

Chaises and chairs in the hotel's colors of sapphire and emerald were arranged to offer ease to sun worshipers or those who preferred the shade.

Seated at one of the glass tables under the jewel tone stripes of a slanted umbrella was Daniel MacGregor.

He got to his feet when he saw her, and Darcy was again struck by the raw power of the man who had lived nearly a century, had built empires, raised a president, stood at the head of a fascinating family.

"Thanks so much for agreeing to see me like this, Mr. MacGregor."

He winked and gallantly pulled out a chair for her. "A pretty woman calls and asks to see me alone, I'd be a fool to say no." He took his seat across from her. Instantly a waiter appeared with a pot of coffee. "Do you want breakfast, lass?"

"No." She smiled weakly. "I'm too nervous to eat."

"Food's just what you need then. Bring the girl some bacon and eggs—you need some meat on you," he said to Darcy. "Scramble the eggs, and don't be stingy with the hash browns. And bring me the same."

"Right away, Mr. MacGregor."

And that, Darcy mused as the waiter scurried away, was likely the typical response of those who came into Daniel MacGregor's orbit. Right away, Mr. MacGregor, and off they rushed to follow orders.

"Now." He picked up his cup. "You'll eat and see if you don't feel steadier. A lot's happened to you in a short time. Anybody'd be a bit rocky. My grandson's taking good care of you?"

"Yes. He's been wonderful. All of you have been wonderful."

"But the ground seems a bit boggy under your feet."

"Yes." Her breath came out in a whoosh of relief that he understood. "It's all so…foreign. Exciting," she added, scanning the lush rooftop garden. "I feel as if I've dropped down into the middle of a book, and I'm vague on the first chapters and don't have any idea how it's going to end."

"Nothing wrong with enjoying the page you're on."

"No, and I have been." Self-consciously she lifted a hand to finger the silver-and-gold twists that dangled from her ear. "But I have to think about what's going to happen when I turn that page. I can't keep buying new clothes and earrings, and living in the moment. Money's a responsibility, isn't it?"

He leaned back, lips pursed as he studied her. Delicate she might look, he mused, but there was nothing delicate about her brain. He had a feeling it was both strong and flexible. All the better, he decided. The wife of his grandson should possess a nimble mind and not a shallow one.

"That it is," he said, and smiled at her.

The smile confused her. It was so…canny. And there were secrets dancing in those bright blue eyes. A little flustered, she picked up her coffee, forgetting to add her customary cream. "There were dozens of calls on my voice mail when I checked it this morning."

"That's to be expected."

"Yes, I know. Mac told me it would happen, but I didn't imagine there would be so many. Reporters…" She laughed a little. "People from magazines I've read, television shows I've watched suddenly want to talk to me. I haven't done anything. I haven't saved a life or found the cure for the common cold or given birth to quintuplets."

His brows shot up. "Do multiple births run in your family?"

"No."

"Pity," he murmured. He'd have enjoyed twin babies. Still, he brushed that aside as Darcy stared at him in confusion. "You've lived a common fantasy. Instant wealth. And you're young, pretty, you come from a small town in the Midwest and you were down to your last dollar. It's a good story. People who read it or hear it can root for you, and imagine it could happen to them."

"Yes, I suppose that's true. It's only fair I talk to some of them." She paused as the waiter returned with two heaping plates. Daunted, Darcy stared down at hers while Daniel dug into his with gusto.

"Eat up, girl. You need some fuel."

She picked up her fork. "I didn't know they served meals up here."

Daniel grinned. "They don't. Just drinks and such as a rule. But it's a fine thing to break the rules now and then. You wanted to be private," he reminded her. "And not many come up here so early in the day. The restaurants inside will likely be packed with people wanting the special buffet and the like."

"There are six restaurants," she told him. "I read about them in the hotel guide. Six. And four swimming pools."

"People have to eat, and some like to be seen around the pool when they're not gambling."

"I can't get over how…huge this place is. Theaters and lounges, the open-air auditorium. It's a maze."

"And all roads lead back to the casino. It's not a casual design," he added with a wink. "Whatever else there is to do in a hotel of this nature, gambling's the hub."

"It's beautiful and exciting. Then you come up here, and you can look beyond it all and see the desert. I love looking at the desert."

"One of the reasons there aren't any windows in the casino. Wouldn't want any distraction." He shot her a warrior's grin. "You should eat a good breakfast, then when it's settled, take yourself a nice swim. I swim most every day. Keeps me young."

It was more than that, Darcy thought. It was the energy, the avid interest in life, the delight in the challenge of it that kept him vital. She was counting on that interest and that delight. "Um…Mr. Mac-Gregor, Caine—gave me a list of names. Financial advisors, brokers, that sort of thing."

Daniel grunted and, since no one was around to stop him, dashed salt on his potatoes. "You need to protect your capital."

"I understand that, particularly since a large percentage of the calls on my voice mail were from people wanting to discuss my finances. One offered to fly me into Los Angeles, put me up at the Beverly Wilshire so that I could take a meeting."

Frowning, she buttered a piece of toast. "Most of them sounded very interested in discussing portfolios and investments, but none of them were on the list your son gave me."

"That doesn't surprise me."

"I wrote them down. I have both lists. I wondered if you would mind looking at them? I know your son prefers giving me a range of choices, but I think I'd do better if I was pointed in a specific direction."

"Let's have a look." Daniel pulled his glasses out of his pocket, perched them on his nose as Darcy took her lists from her purse. "Ha! Vultures, fly-by-nights. Grifters." With barely a glance he slapped the first list facedown. "You'll want to stay away from these, lass."

She nodded. "That's what I thought. That's the list of the ones who called. This is the one your son gave me."

He tapped his fingers on the table as he read the second list. "The boy learned, didn't he?" Pleased with the names Caine had offered, Daniel scratched his chin through his beard. "Any one of these would do well for you. The best thing is for you to interview the top man at each firm, get a feel for it. Let them woo you, then trust your gut."

She was already trusting her gut but wasn't quite ready to tell him what she wanted. "I've never had any money, never had more to worry about—and over—than what I could juggle in my checking account month to month. Last night, I tried to imagine what a million dollars would look like. I couldn't. And now, even after taxes, I have a bit more than what I can't even imagine."

Daniel poured himself a second cup of coffee. Anna would scalp him, he thought with delight, if she knew he was slurping up that much caffeine. "Tell me what you want from your money."

From it, she thought. Not what she wanted to

do with it, but what she wanted from it. "Time," she said immediately. "Time enough so that I can do what I've always wanted to do. I've always wanted to write, and always had to steal the time to do it. I want that first, the time to finish my new book, then time to start the next," she said with a smile. "Because I want to be a writer, and the only way to be one is to write."

"Are you any good at it?"

"Yes, I am. It's the only thing I've ever really been good at, really felt confident about. I just need another few weeks to finish the one I'm working on."

"The money'll buy you more than a few weeks."

"I know. I intend to have fun with it, too." Her eyes glinted as she leaned forward. "I'm starting to realize that fun wasn't a big part of my life. I'm going to correct that. Whoever said money couldn't buy happiness must have been happy to begin with. Because if it can't, at least it can buy the opportunity to explore being happy." She laughed and settled back. "I'm going to explore being happy, Mr. MacGregor."

"That's a sensible thing."

"Yes, I think it is. Being happy isn't something I'm going to take for granted," she said quietly, "or something I intend to waste."

He laid his big hand over hers. "Have you been so unhappy?"

"I suppose in some ways I have been." She moved her shoulders restlessly. "But I have a chance now to make choices, for myself. It makes all the difference in the world. So I want to make good choices."

"I think you will." He gave her hand a squeeze and a pat. "You've already started to."

"I want to use the money well. And I want to give some back."

"To my grandson?"

"Oh." She laughed again and propped her elbows on the table. "In the casino. Yes, indeed. That's part of the fun, isn't it? But I meant to give some of that money, that time and that opportunity to explore happiness back. I want to make a donation, to literacy, I think. It fits, doesn't it?"

"Aye." He reached out to pat her cheek. "It fits, and you wear it well."

"I don't know how it's done, though. I thought you would."

"I'd be happy to help you with it." When the waiter came to remove their plates, Daniel waved a hand. "Leave hers," he ordered. "She hasn't eaten enough. Now," he continued as Darcy and the waiter exchanged resigned glances, "you'll have your time, your opportunity, and you'll have given something back. Unless you intend to toss around money like confetti, and you don't strike me as an idiot, you'll have quite a bit left over. What do you want from that?"

She bit her lip, easing forward. "More," she said, then blinked when he threw back his head and roared with laughter.

"Now there's a lass with a head on her shoulders. I knew it."

"It sounds greedy, but—"

"It sounds sane," he corrected. "Why should you want less? More is better, after all. You want your money to work for you. I'd call you a fool if you wanted otherwise."

"Mr. MacGregor." She took a deep breath and

rolled the dice. "I want you to take my money and make it work for me."

The blue eyes narrowed. "Do you now? And why is that?"

"Because it seems to me I'd be a fool to settle for less than the best."

His eyes remained narrowed, fixed on her face so intensely she felt heat rising to her cheeks. Certain she'd gone too far, she started to babble an apology.

Then the mouth surrounded by that white beard began to curve. "Neither of us are fools, are we, lass?"

"No, sir."

"Well then." Grinning, his eyes sparkling with challenge, he twisted the gold knob on his cane. When it hinged back, he slipped out a thick cigar. With the lighter he took out of his pocket, he touched tip of flame reverently to tip of cigar, his bright eyes closing in pleasure as he took the first puffs.

"I know it's a lot to ask, Mr. MacGregor, but—"

"Daniel," he said, and grinned fiercely. "We're

partners, aren't we? Eat," he ordered when Darcy only stared at him. "I've a couple ideas for how to get you that 'more' you'd like. Are you a gambler, little girl?"

With her head light and her heart soaring, Darcy bit into a piece of bacon. "It looks like I am."

Mac had a lot on his mind. The media was executing a full-court press, scrambling for access to Darcy. Reporters were wild for interviews and personal data. The morning editions, both local and national had played variations on the theme.

Little Darcy From Kansas Hits Yellow Brick Road

From Kansas To Oz On Three-Dollar Bet

Over The Rainbow With A Million For Kansas Librarian

Normally he would have been amused, and certainly pleased at the positive publicity the story generated for Comanche Vegas. Reservations in the hotel were soaring, and he had no doubt that the casino would be three deep at the slots and tables as long as the story was hot.

He could handle the demands on his time, the incessant requests for interviews and photos. He could add staff to each shift, and intended to work the floor himself during peak periods. In fact, his parents had already agreed to extend their stay a few days and pitch in. And he preferred, just now, to have his plate overfull.

God knows he needed the distraction to keep his mind off his libido. It was suddenly and insistently on edge due to one small, big-eyed woman with a shy smile.

He wasn't inclined toward a serious relationship and certainly didn't intend to become involved with an innocent, naive woman who didn't know the difference between a straight and a flush.

He considered himself a disciplined man who knew how to control his baser instincts and resist temptations. He didn't play at love like his brother, Duncan. Nor did he consider it a pesky fly to be swatted aside like his sister Amelia. And he certainly had no intention of settling down and raising a family at this stage of his life as his sister Gwen was doing.

For Mac love was something to be dealt with eventually, when there was time, when the odds were favorable and when there was a good chance of raking in all the chips.

He wanted what his parents had. Perhaps he hadn't realized that quite so clearly until Darcy had pointed out just what they did have together. But he could admit he had always used them as his yardstick where relationships were concerned.

It was undoubtedly the reason he'd avoided any long-term or serious ones up to this point.

He enjoyed women, but involvement beyond a certain level led to complications, and complications invariably led to hurt on one side or the other. He'd been very careful not to hurt any of the women who had brushed in and out of his life.

He had no intention of breaking that particular rule now.

As far as Darcy Wallace was concerned, he'd decided it was a bad bet all around. She was too inexperienced, too vulnerable.

He was setting her firmly off-limits. Friendship, he ordered himself. A steadying hand until she had her feet firmly under her, and nothing more.

Then he stepped onto the rooftop garden and saw her. She was sitting at one of the tables, her big, elfin eyes wide and intent on his grandfather's face. Their heads were close together, like conspirators, he thought, and wondered what the hell was going on between them.

She looked so…fragile, he decided, so slimly built with those pretty, ringless hands clasped together like a schoolgirl's. She'd worked a foot out of one strappy sandal, and was waving the shoe by a single strap hooked around toes painted a soft shell pink.

The image that flashed through his mind of nibbling on those pretty toes and working his way up those slender legs had him muttering a curse.

Lust, something he normally accepted and enjoyed, was currently driving him mad.

Irritation still simmered in his eyes as he stepped through the palms and up to the table. Daniel leaned back, beamed and wiggled his eyebrows. "Well, there's a likely lad. Want some coffee, boy?"

"I could do with a cup." Because he knew Daniel well, Mac didn't trust him a whit. He scraped back a chair, straddled it and met his grandfather's cheerful gaze. "What's going on here?"

"Why, I'm having breakfast with this pretty young thing, which you'd be doing yourself if you weren't slow-witted."

"I've got a casino to run," Mac said shortly, and turned his sharp eyes to Darcy. "Did you get some rest?"

"Yes, plenty, thank you." She jolted when Daniel thumped his fist on the table.

"God Almighty, boy, is that any way to greet a woman in the morning? Why aren't you telling her how pretty she looks, or asking her if she'll take a drive with you this evening?"

"I'm working this evening," Mac said mildly.

"The day a MacGregor can't find time for a sweet-eyed woman is a sorry day. A sorry day, indeed. You'd like a drive, wouldn't you, lass, up into the hills in the moonlight?"

"I—yes, but—"

"There." Daniel thumped his fist again. "Are you going to do something about this, boy, or do I have to hang my head in shame?"

Considering, Mac picked up the cigar smol-

dering in the ashtray. He studied it thoughtfully, turned it in his hand. "And what's this?"
Lifting his brow, Mac smiled thinly at his
grandfather. "This wouldn't be yours, would it,
Grandpa?"

Daniel's gaze slid away. He studied his own
fingernails intently. "I don't know what you're
talking about. Now—"

"Grandma would be very displeased if she
thought you were sneaking cigars behind her back
again." Idly Mac tapped the ash. "Very displeased."

"It's mine," Darcy blurted out, and both men
turned to stare at her.

"Yours?" Mac said in a voice that dripped
like honey.

"Yes." She jerked her shoulder in what she
hoped was an arrogant shrug. "So what?"

"So…" Mac's teeth flashed in a grin. "Enjoy,"
he suggested, and handed her the cigar.

The challenge in his eyes left her little choice.
Defiantly she took a puff. Her head spun, her
throat closed, but she managed to muffle most of
the cough. "It's very smooth." She wheezed as
she choked on smoke.

Her eyes teared as she gamefully puffed again. Mac had to resist an urge to tug her into his lap and nuzzle her. "I can see that. Want a brandy to go with it?"

"Not before lunch." She coughed again, felt her stomach pitch. "Your grandfather—" She coughed, blinked away tears. "Your grandfather and I were discussing business."

"Don't let me stop you. Done with this?" He picked up a slice of her bacon. He bit in neatly then grinned. She was turning a very interesting shade of green. "Put that down, darling, before you pass out."

"I'm perfectly fine."

"You're a rare one, Darcy." Adoring her, Daniel rose. He tipped up her chin, kissed her full on the mouth. "I'll get started on that business we were speaking of." He sent his grandson a glowering look. "Don't shame me, Robbie."

"Who's Robbie?" Darcy asked dizzily when Daniel strode off.

"I am, to him, occasionally."

"Oh." She smiled. "That's sweet."

"You're going to make yourself sick," Mac muttered, and took the cigar from her fingers. "I didn't think you'd do it."

She let her reeling head fall back. "I don't know what you're talking about."

With a sigh, Mac picked up her water glass and held it to her lips. "Did you really think I'd rat on him? Come on, sip a little. The smoke's made you punchy."

"It's not so bad. I kind of like it." She turned her head to smile at him. "You wouldn't have told? About the cigar."

"It wouldn't have mattered. My grandmother knows he sneaks them every chance he gets."

"I wish he were my grandfather. I think he's the most wonderful man in the world."

"He likes you, too. Steady now?"

"I'm fine." She studied what was left of the cigar as it smoked in the ashtray. "I may just take it up." But she drank the water again to cool her throat. "He shouldn't have teased you that way, about taking me for a drive."

With a few deliberate taps, Mac put out the cigar. "He's decided you suit me."

"Oh." The idea wound through her mind, then warmed her heart. "Really?"

"The MacGregor's fondest wish is to see all of his grandchildren married and producing babies. And the more he has to do with it, the better. He actually arranged for my sister, and two of my cousins to meet men he'd specifically picked out for them."

"What happened?"

"In those cases, it worked, which only makes him more difficult to control. He's on a streak. And just now…" He angled his head, skimmed his gaze over her face. "He's decided you'll do for me."

"I see." She supposed the quick thrill and sense of glee was inappropriate. But it was very hard to control the curve of her lips. "I'm flattered."

"So you should be. I am, after all, the oldest grandchild—and he's a fussy man when it comes to family."

"But it irritates you."

"Mildly," he admitted. "As much as I love him, I've no intention of going along with his grand schemes. I apologize if he got you out here this morning to put ideas in your head, but I'm not looking for marriage."

Her eyes went wide and dark. "Excuse me?"

"I suspected, when I was told the two of you were together up here, that he'd been planting seeds."

The warmth that had settled inside her iced over and went rock hard. "And, of course, someone like me would be fertile ground for such seeds."

Her tone was so quiet, so pleasant, he missed the flash. "He can't help it. And your name being Wallace put a cap on it. Strong Scot blood," he said with a grin and a burr. "He'd consider you tailor-made to bear my children."

"And since you're not in the market for a wife or children, you thought it only fair to nip in the bud any ideas he might have planted in my vulnerable mind in that area."

He caught the underlying frost in the tone now. "More or less," he agreed, cautiously. "Darcy—"

"You arrogant, self-important, *insulting* son of a bitch." She sprang to her feet so abruptly the table jerked. The water glass toppled over and crashed on the tiles as she stood vibrating with temper, her fists clenched and eyes blazing. "I'm not the empty-headed, dim-witted, *needy* fool you seem to think I am."

"That's not what I meant." More than a little wary, he got to his feet. "That's not at all what I meant."

"Don't stand there and tell me what you didn't mean. I know perfectly well when I'm being considered a corn-for-brains moron. You're not the first who's made that mistake, but I swear to God, you're going to be the last. I'm perfectly aware that you don't want me."

"I never said—"

"Do you think I don't know I'm not your type?" Furious, she shoved the chair into the table, and sent another glass crashing. "You prefer big-busted showgirls with eight feet of leg and yards of hair."

"What? Where the hell did that come from?"

Straight out of her dream the night before, but she'd be damned if she'd tell him. "I don't have any delusions about you. Just because I would have slept with you doesn't mean I expected you to sweep me off to the altar. If all I wanted was marriage, I could have stayed exactly where I was."

She still looked like a fairy, he noted, one who could—and would—spitefully turn an incautious man into a braying jackass. "Before you break any more glassware, let me apologize." He put a restraining hand on the back of the chair before she could jam it into the table again. "I didn't want my grandfather to put you in an uncomfortable position."

"You've accomplished that all on your own." Mortification mixed with temper to send her color high. "It may surprise you to know that I asked Daniel to meet me here this morning, and— though it may crush your outrageous ego—it had nothing whatsoever to do with you. It was a business meeting," she said rather grandly.

"Business?" He squinted against the sun. "What sort of business?"

"I don't believe that's any of your concern," she told him coldly. "But since you'll undoubtedly harass Daniel over it, I'll tell you. Daniel has agreed to be my financial advisor."

Intrigued, Mac slipped his hands into his

pockets and rocked on his heels. "You asked him to handle your money?"

"Is there any reason I shouldn't?"

"No." Hoping to cool her off a bit, he smiled and inclined his head. "You couldn't do better."

"Precisely."

And he, Mac thought, couldn't have done any worse. "Darcy—"

"I don't want your apology." Her voice glittered with ice. "I don't want your excuses or your pitiful reasons. I believe we both understand perfectly well the status of our relationship." She snatched up her purse. "You can bill me for the cost of the glasses."

He couldn't stop the wince as she stormed off, slapping her way though the palms. He had both feet up to the knees in his mouth, he decided, grimacing at the sparkle of shattered glass on the tiles.

Getting them out would be the first problem, he thought.

The second problem would be a great deal more complex.

Just how was he going to deal with the fact that the woman who had just ripped the skin off his hide utterly fascinated him?

Chapter Eight

For the next two days Darcy concentrated on her writing. For the first time in her life, she decided, she was going to do what she wanted, when she wanted. If she wanted to work until three in the morning and sleep until noon, there was no one to criticize her habits. Dinner at midnight? Why not?

It was her life now, and sometime during those first furious hours, she realized she was finally living it.

She was going to miss Daniel, she thought. He'd returned East the day before, with a promise to keep in close contact on the investments he was making for her. He'd issued an open invitation for her to visit his home in Hyannis Port.

Darcy intended to take him up on it. She'd grown very fond of the MacGregors. They were warm, generous and delightful people—even if one particular member of the clan was arrogant, insulting and infuriating.

He actually thought sending her flowers was going to make up for it. She sniffed as she glanced over at the lush arrangement of three dozen silvery white roses she'd instructed the bellman to place on the conference table. They were the most beautiful flowers she'd ever seen—which he undoubtedly knew, she thought, hardening her heart as she sat at the desk.

She hadn't acknowledged them, or the sweet basket of button-eyed daisies that stood perkily on her bathroom counter, or the vase of stunning tropical blooms that graced the bureau in the bedroom.

The roses had come first, she remembered, tapping her fingers on the desk. Barely an hour after she'd stormed back into her room after the conversation with Mac, the bellman had knocked on her door. The note with them had been a smooth apology she'd easily ignored.

It was no one's business but hers that she'd tucked the card away in her lingerie drawer.

The daisies had come the next day, with a request that she call him when she had a moment. She'd tucked that card away too, and had ignored the request—just as she'd ignored his insistent knocking at her door the previous evening.

This morning it was birds-of-paradise and hibiscus with a much pithier request.

Damn it, Darcy. Open the door.

With a short, humorless laugh, she turned on her laptop. She would *not* open the door, not to him. Not the literal door of her room, or the metaphorical door to her heart. It wasn't simply mortifying that she'd allowed herself to fall in love with him, it was…typical, she thought and clenched her teeth.

Pitiful, lonely woman meets sophisticated, handsome man and tumbles face-first at his feet.

Well, she'd picked herself up now, hadn't she? He could send her an acre of flowers, a ream of notes, but it wasn't going to change a thing.

She had her direction now. As soon as she completed the draft of her book, she was going to a realtor. She intended to buy a house—something big and sand colored that faced the open mystery of the desert and the majestic ring of mountains.

Something with a pool, she decided, and skylights. She'd always wanted skylights.

Settling here had nothing to do with Mac, she told herself. She liked it here. She liked the hot winds, the sprawling desert, the pulse of life and promise that beat in the air. Las Vegas was the fastest growing city in the U.S., wasn't it, and reported to be one of the most livable?

It said so in the glossy hotel guide on her coffee table.

Why shouldn't she live here?

When the phone rang she merely scowled at it. If it was Mac thinking she was the least bit interested in speaking to him, he could think again. She ignored the call, rolled her shoulders once, then dove back into the story.

Mac prowled his office restlessly while his mother scanned the printout of bookings for the next six months. "You've got a wonderful lineup here."

"Mmm." He couldn't concentrate, and it infuriated him.

He'd only wanted to warn her about his grandfather's tendency for plots and schemes. For her own good, he thought, moving from window to window as if to improve his view. And he'd apologized repeatedly. She didn't even have the courtesy to acknowledge it.

He'd come close, far too close, to using his passkey and circumventing the control on her private elevator. And that, he reminded himself would have been an unforgivable invasion of her privacy and a breach of his responsibilities to The Comanche.

But what the hell was she doing in that suite? She hadn't had a meal outside of it since that breakfast on the roof. She hadn't stepped foot in the casino, or any of the lounges.

Sulking. It was so unattractive, he decided, and sulked a bit himself.

"It serves me right for trying to look after her," he muttered.

"What?" Serena glanced over, then shook her head. She knew very well she'd had only the stingiest slice of her son's attention for the past hour. "Mac, what's wrong?"

"Nothing's wrong. Do you want to see the entertainment schedule?"

She lifted her eyebrows and waved the printout. "I'm looking at it."

"Oh. Right." He turned to scowl out the window again.

With a sigh, Serena set the papers aside. "You might as well tell me what's bothering you. I'll just nag you until you do anyway."

"Who'd have thought she could be so stubborn?" The words exploded out of his mouth as he whirled back. "If she can be this damn perverse, how the hell did she get pushed around so much?"

Serena hummed in her throat then, crossing her legs, settled back. Women rarely ruffled Mac, she mused, and took it as a very good sign. "I assume you're talking about Darcy."

"Of course, I'm talking about Darcy." Frustration simmered in his eyes. "I don't know what the hell she's doing, locked in that suite day and night."

"Writing."

"What do you mean writing?"

"Her book," Serena said patiently. "She's trying to finish the first draft of her book. She wants to have that done before she starts querying agents."

"How do you know?"

"Because she told me. We had tea in her suite yesterday."

It took monumental control to keep his mouth from falling open. "She let you in?"

"Of course, she let me in. I talked her into taking a short break from it. She's a very disciplined young woman, and very determined on this. And talented."

"Talented?"

"I persuaded her to let me read a few pages of the book she'd finished last year." Serena's lips curved up into a pleased smile. "I was impressed. And entertained. Does that surprise you?"

"No." He realized it didn't, not in the least. "So she's working."

"That's right."

"That's no excuse for being rude."

"Rude? Darcy?"

"I'm tired of the silent treatment," he muttered.

"She's not speaking to you? What did you do?"

Mac set his teeth and shot a withering look at Serena. "Why do you assume I did anything?"

"Darling." She rose, crossing over to lay a hand on his cheek. "As much as I love you, you're a man. Now, what did you do to upset her?"

"I was simply trying to explain The Mac-Gregor to her. I came across them with their heads together, and Grandpa started in on why didn't I take this pretty young girl for a drive in the moonlight. You know the routine."

"Yes, I do." Daniel "Subtle" MacGregor, she thought with a windy sigh. "Exactly how were you trying to explain him to her?"

"I told her he wanted his grandchildren married, settled and producing more little Mac-Gregors, that it appeared he'd picked her out for me. I apologized for him, and explained that I wasn't looking for marriage, and she shouldn't take him too seriously."

Serena stepped back, the better to stare at her firstborn. "And you used to be such a bright child."

"I was only thinking of her," he retorted. "I thought he was setting her up. How was I supposed to know she'd asked him to meet her on business? I admit I put my foot in it." He jammed his hands into his pockets. "I apologized, several times. I sent her flowers, I've called—not that she'll answer the damn phone. What the devil am I supposed to do? Grovel?"

"It might be good for you," Serena murmured, then laughed as he hissed at her. "Mac." Gently she cupped her hands on his face. "Why are you so worried about it? Do you have feelings for her?"

"I care what happens to her. She stumbled in here like a refugee, for God's sake. She needs someone to look out for her."

She kept her eyes level on his. "So your feelings for her are…brotherly."

He hesitated just a moment too long. "They should be."

"Are they?"

"I don't know."

Loving him, she skimmed her fingers back into his hair. "Maybe you should find out."

"How? She won't talk to me."

"A man who has both MacGregor and Blade blood in his veins wouldn't let something like a locked door stop him for long." She smiled, kissed him firmly. "My money's on you."

Darcy's eyes were closed as she tried to visualize the scene before letting the words come. Now, finally, though danger shadowed every corner, her two main characters would come together. No longer would they resist this vital and primitive pull, no longer would needs that swam in the blood and slammed in the heart be denied. It was now. Had to be now.

The room was cold and smelled of damp the blazing fire had yet to conquer. The blue haze of a winter moon slipped through the windows.

He would touch her. How would he touch her? A brush of knuckles on her cheek? Her breath would catch, strangle in her throat, shudder through her lips. Would she feel the heat of his body as he drew her close? What would be the last thing running through her mind in those seconds just before his mouth lowered, took possession of hers?

Insanity, Darcy thought. And she would welcome it.

Keeping her eyes closed, Darcy let the words run through her mind and onto the page. The sudden shrill of the phone was so abrupt and out of place in her chilly cabin in the mountains, she snatched it up without thinking.

"Yes, yes, hello?"

"Darcy." The voice was grave, undeniably irritated, and all too familiar.

"Gerald." The passion and promise of the scene vanished, replaced by nerves. "Ah, how are you?"

"How would you expect me to be? You've caused me a great deal of trouble."

"I'm sorry." The apology was automatic, making her wince the moment it was out of her mouth.

"I can't imagine what you were thinking of. We'll discuss it. Give me your room number."

"My room number?" Nerves shot directly to panic. "Where are you?"

"I'm in the lobby of this ridiculous place you chose to land in. It's beyond inappropriate—

which I should have expected given your recent behavior. But we'll straighten it out shortly. Your room number, Darcy?"

Her room? Her haven. No, no, she couldn't let him invade her sanctuary. "I—I'll come down," she said quickly. "There's a seating area near the waterfall. It's on the left of the reception desk in the main lobby. Do you see it?"

"I could hardly miss it, could I? Don't dawdle."

"No, I'll be right down."

She hung up, pushed away from the desk. Despair closed in and was resolutely fought back. He couldn't make her do anything she didn't want to do, she reminded herself. He had no power here, no control. He had nothing that she didn't give him.

But the hand that picked up her purse wasn't completely steady. Her legs wanted badly to shake as she walked to the elevator. She concentrated on keeping her knees from knocking together all the way down.

The lobby was crowded with people, families of tourists who wandered through to toss coins into the pool at the base of the waterfall or to see the live-action show in the open-air amphitheater. Guests checked in, checked out. Others were lured by the ching of slots and headed for the casino.

Gerald sat in one of the curved-back chairs near the bubbling pool. His dark suit was without a wrinkle, his hard, handsome face without a smile as he scanned the activity around him with a glint of derision in his dark eyes.

He looked successful, Darcy thought. Removed from the chaotic whirl around him. Cold, she decided. It was his cold nature that had always frightened her.

His head turned as she approached. Even as his eyes skimmed over her, registering both surprise and disapproval of her choice of pale green shorts and a peach blouse, he got to his feet.

Manners, she thought. He'd always had excellent manners.

"I assume you have an explanation for all of this." He gestured to a chair.

The gesture, she mused, was just one of the ways he took control. *Sit, Darcy.* And she'd always quietly obeyed.

This time she stood.

"I decided to relocate."

"Don't be absurd." He dismissed this with a wave of his hand before taking her arm and pulling her firmly into a chair. "Do you have any idea what embarrassment you've caused me? Sneaking out of town in the middle of the night—"

"I didn't sneak." Of course she had, she thought.

He merely arched a brow, adult to child. "You left without a word to anyone. You've been irresponsible, which again, I should have expected. Taking a trip like this without any planning. What did you expect to accomplish?"

Escape, she thought. Adventure. Life. She linked her fingers together, laid them in her lap and tried to speak calmly. "I wasn't taking a trip. I was leaving. There's nothing for me in Trader's Corners."

"It's your home."

"Not anymore."

"Don't be more foolish than necessary. Do you have any idea what sort of position you've put me in? I find my fiancée gone—"

"I'm not your fiancée, Gerald. I broke our engagement some time ago."

His gaze never wavered. "And I've been more than patient, giving you time to come to your senses and calm your nerves. This is how you behave. Las Vegas, for pity's sake."

He placed his hands neatly on his knees and leaned forward. "People are gossiping about you now. And that reflects poorly on me. You've been splashed all over the national news—some sort of three-day wonder."

"I won nearly two million dollars. That's news."

"Gambling." He sneered on the word, then leaned back again. "I'll handle the press, of course. The interest will die down soon enough, and it's a simple matter to put a positive spin on the incident, to play down the sordid."

"Sordid? I put money into a slot machine. I hit the jackpot. What's sordid about it?"

He spared her a weary glance. "I wouldn't expect you to understand the underlying thrust of this, Darcy. Your innocence, at least, does you credit. We'll arrange for the money to be transferred—"

"No." Her heart was beginning to pound in her throat.

"You can hardly leave it in Nevada. My broker will invest it properly. We'll see that you get a nice allowance from the interest."

An allowance, she thought, through the dull buzzing in her head. As if she were a child who could be indulged with carefully controlled spending money. "It's already being invested. Mr. MacGregor, Daniel MacGregor is handling it."

Shock reflected in his eyes as his hand shot out to grip hers. "My God, Darcy, you're not telling me you've given over a million dollars to a stranger?"

"He's not a stranger. And actually, he has slightly under a million for now. There are taxes and living expenses to consider."

"How could you be so stupid?" His voice rose, making her cringe back from it, and the disgusted fury in his eyes. "Put it together—a simpleton could see it. MacGregor has a financial interest in this hotel. And now he has the money you took from this hotel."

"I'm not stupid," Darcy said in a quiet voice. "And Daniel MacGregor isn't a thief."

"My lawyer will draw up the necessary papers to transfer the funds—what there are left of them. We'll have to work quickly." He glanced at his watch. "I'll have to call him at home. Inconvenient, but it can't be helped. Go up and pack while I deal with this latest mess you've made. The sooner I get home, the sooner this can be mended."

"Did you come for the money or for me, Gerald?" She flexed her hand in his, then let it lie passively. She would never win in a physical altercation so she concentrated her efforts, and her anger, into the verbal. "It occurs to me that your pattern would have been to call and order me home once you knew where I was. You wouldn't have bothered to rearrange your busy schedule and come in person. You wouldn't have felt the need. You'd have been so sure I'd have tucked my tail between my legs and come back when you snapped your fingers."

"I don't have time for this now, Darcy. Go pack, and change into something suitable for travel."

"I'm not going anywhere."

Fury had his fingers biting into hers as he jerked her to her feet. "Do what you're told. Now. I will not tolerate a public scene."

"Then leave, because you're about to get one."

A hand dropped lightly onto her shoulder. She knew before he spoke that it was Mac. "Is there a problem here?"

"No." She didn't look at him, couldn't. "Gerald, this is Mac Blade. He runs The Comanche. Mac, Gerald was just leaving."

"Goodbye, Gerald," Mac said in a mild tone that flashed just around the edges. "I believe the lady would like her hand back."

"Neither Darcy nor I require your interference."

Mac stepped forward until they were eye-to-eye. "I haven't begun to interfere, but I'd be happy to." His smile was lethal. "In fact, I've been looking forward to the opportunity."

"Don't." More angry than frightened now, Darcy pushed her way between them. "I'm perfectly capable of handling my own problems."

"Is this what you've been up to, Darcy?" Disgust laced Gerald's voice as he stared down at her. "Letting yourself be seduced by this…

person? Deluding yourself that he would want anything more from you than to cheat you out of the money you took from him, and some cheap sex on the side?"

She felt the ripple behind her, sensed that Mac was braced to attack, and quickly swung her hands back to grip his arms. "Please, don't. Please." The muscles seemed to vibrate against her restraining fingers. "It won't help. Please."

She ignored the interested onlookers who were busy pretending not to watch. Perhaps it helped, just a little, that her back was firmly pressed against the solid wall of Mac's chest. But she knew she had to stand on her own now, or she'd never manage to do so.

"Gerald, what I do, where I do it and with whom has nothing whatever to do with you. I apologize for ever agreeing to marry you. It was a mistake I tried to rectify, but you never wanted to hear me. Other than that, I have nothing to be sorry for."

She drew a fresh, steadying breath while she watched his jaw clench. He wanted to hit her, she realized, and found she wasn't surprised. If she hadn't found the courage to run, he would have ended up using fists, as well as words. Sooner or later, intimidation wouldn't have been enough.

The certainty of that gave her the will to finish it. "You maneuvered and manipulated me, because you could. And that's why you wanted to marry me—at first anyway. After that, you insisted on it because you couldn't and wouldn't accept some little no one refusing you—and having to explain a broken engagement to the neighbors."

His face had gone stone cold. "I'm not going to stand here while you air our personal business in public."

"You're free to leave anytime. You came here because I'm suddenly some little no one with a great deal of money. That ups the stakes—and so does the press. I'm sure a few enterprising reporters have made their way to Trader's Corners, and it wouldn't take much for any of them to dig up that we'd once been engaged. Embarrassing for you, but it can't be helped.

"I'm telling you now, as clearly as I know how, that you'll never get your hands on me or my money. That I'm never coming back. I live here now, and I like it. I don't like you, and I realize I never have."

He stepped back from her abruptly. "I can see now that you're not the person I believed you to be."

"I can't tell you how happy that makes me. Cut your losses, Gerald," she said quietly. "And go home."

He angled his head, studying both her and Mac with equal disdain. "As far as I can see, the two of you are well suited to each other, and this place. If you mention my name in the media, I'll be forced to take legal action."

"Don't worry," Darcy murmured as he strode away. "I seem to have forgotten your name already."

"Well done." Unable to resist, Mac lowered his head and pressed a kiss to the top of hers.

She only closed her eyes. "However it was done, it's over. Thanks for offering to help."

"You didn't appear to need it." But she was starting to tremble now. "Let me take you upstairs."

"I know the way."

"Darcy." He turned her around, leaving his hands on her shoulders. "You wouldn't give me the satisfaction of breaking his face. You owe me."

She drummed up something that passed for a smile. "All right. I always pay my debts."

He kept an arm around her shoulders as he walked her to the elevator. Instinctively he rubbed a hand up and down her arm to ease the trembling. "Did you get my flowers?"

"Yes, they're very nice." Her voice went prim, pleasing him. "Thank you."

He used his passkey to access her floor. "My mother tells me you've been working."

"That's right."

"So…the reason you haven't answered my calls—or let me into your room is because you've been busy writing. Not because you hold a grudge."

She shifted uncomfortably. "I don't hold grudges. Usually."

"But you're making an exception for me."

"I suppose."

"Okay. You've got two choices. You can forgive me for being…I believe 'arrogant' and 'insulting' was the way you put it, or I'm going to be forced to go after Gerald and pound my frustrations out on him."

"You wouldn't do that."

"Oh yes." He smiled darkly. "I would."

She stared at him even after the elevator doors slid open. "You would," she realized with something between shock and horrified delight. "It wouldn't solve anything."

"But I'd enjoy it so much. So are you going to invite me inside, or do I go find him?"

She jerked a shoulder and tried not to be pleased. "Come in. I'm probably too distracted to work anyway."

"Thanks." He glanced toward her desk. "How's it going?"

"Very well."

"My mother said you let her read a couple pages."

"She made it hard to say no. Would you like a drink? Some coffee?"

"Nothing right now. Are you going to let me read some of your book?"

"When it's published you can read the whole thing."

He shifted his gaze from the desk to her face. Her color was back, which relieved him. She'd looked much too pale, and much too fragile, downstairs. "I can make it hard to say no, too. It runs in the family. But you're a little shaky at the moment, so I'll wait."

"It's just a reaction." She cupped her elbows in her palms. "I was afraid when he called."

"But you went down and met him."

"It had to be done."

"You could have called me. You didn't have to do it alone."

"Yes, I did. I had to know I could. It seems foolish now to realize I'd ever been intimidated by him. He's so pathetic, really." She hadn't understood that before, she thought now. Hadn't seen the sorry man under the bully. "Still, if I hadn't been, I might not be here. I might not have met you. I have to be grateful for that."

She clasped her hands together. "I appreciate you not hitting him after he insulted you that way."

His eyes stayed on her face. "I wouldn't have hit him for me."

New emotions swam into her eyes. "I knew,

when you came, it would be all right. That I would be all right. And I wasn't afraid anymore. He thought that we've been... I was glad he did, because I'd never let him touch me. And he thinks you have."

He knew it was a mistake to cross to her. The odds were weighted wrong for both of them. "He'll stew about that for a long time. It's almost as good as beating him senseless."

The warmth spreading in her chest was nearly painful. "I'm glad you were there."

"So am I. Are we friends again?"

His knuckles brushed her cheek, made her breath catch, strangle in her throat and shudder through her lips. "Is that what you want to be?"

Her eyes were wide and dark. Her lips parted, full of anticipation, invitation. And irresistible. "Not entirely," he murmured and lowered his mouth to hers.

She knew now what thoughts scrambled through the brain in those last seconds before the mating of lips. Wild and desperate images so bold and tangled they had no name. She stretched up to her toes, her body pressing into his, her hands streaking up his chest to grip his shoulders as she let herself tumble into those shockingly bright colors and shapes.

Her mouth was so eager, so soft and warm and giving. He wanted more of it. Her body was so slight, so pliant, so ready. He wanted all of it. The need was huge, raw as a groan, and forced him to fight for control.

"Darcy—" He started to ease her away, swore that he would, but her arms wound around his neck.

"Please." Her voice was husky, a tremble of urgency. "Oh, please. Touch me."

The whispered request was as seductive as a rustle of black silk. Desire swarmed through him, roaring in his head, throbbing in his loins. "Touching won't be enough."

"You can have enough." She could drown in need, she thought frantically. Already she was going under. "Make love with me." Her voice sounded desperate and very faraway as her lips raced over his face, melted onto his. "Take me to bed."

It was as much demand as offer. Everything inside him responded to both. "I want you." He tore his mouth from hers to press it to her throat. "It's insane how much I want you."

"I don't want to be sane. I don't want you to be. Just once—be with me."

He let the wheel spin. He swept her up in his arms and watched her eyes turn gold with awareness. The fact that she weighed little more than a child terrified him. "I won't hurt you."

"I don't care."

But he did. He nuzzled a sigh from her as he carried her to the stairs and started up. "The first time I brought you up here, I wondered about you. Who is she? Where does she come from?" He laid her on the bed, stroked his fingers down the column of her throat. "What am I going to do with her? I still haven't figured it out."

"When I woke up and saw you, I thought I was dreaming." She lifted a hand to his cheek. "Part of me still does."

He turned his head to press his lips into the cup of her palm. "I'll stop if you ask me." He took her mouth again, going deep, sinking in. "For God's sake, don't ask me."

How could she? Why would she, when nerves

and pleasure and needs were dancing just under her skin? The spread was slick under her back, and his hands were already stroking small, separate fires into life over her body. His mouth drew and drew and drew from hers as if she contained some life force he craved.

Craved.

No one had ever made her feel wanted like this.

His fingers trailed over her as though he found her delicate, special. And when his hand closed over her breast, molded it, her mind emptied.

She was unbearably responsive, her body arching, giving, inviting him to do as he wished. Gently, he ordered himself, go gently here. He blurred her mind, and his, with kisses as he opened her blouse and began to explore warm, smooth flesh.

Her trembles aroused him, almost brutally. Every quiver of her muscles was a miracle to be exploited, then savored. For he found he could savor, the texture of that skin curving subtly above the cup of her bra, the flavor of her throat where the pulse beat so hard and fast.

He drew her up, nibbling tortuously at her mouth as he slipped her blouse aside.

Hesitantly she reached for the buttons of his shirt. She wanted to touch him, to see. To know. A sound of dizzy delight escaped her when she saw her white hands against the dusky gold of his chest.

So strong, she thought, fascinated by the ridge of muscles under her fingertips. So hard and strong and male. Thrilled, she leaned forward to press her lips to his shoulder, to absorb the taste.

He felt something like a growl working through him and pushed down a sudden, violent need to devour. Instead he took her face in his hands, watching her, drinking her in even as his mouth took hers again. Watching still, for those flickers of surprise and pleasure in her eyes, as he slipped her bra aside, as he cupped her breasts in his hands, skimmed his thumbs over nipples that went hot and stiff.

Then he laid her back to capture one sensitized point with his mouth.

Her hand fisted in the spread, dragging at it as hot, liquid sensation flooded her system. A pulse was pounding between her legs, all but burning there. She heard her own moan, a wanton, throaty sound of pleasure as she wrapped around him, racked by edgy, questing needs.

"Easy." He wasn't certain if he were calming her or himself. But her restless movements beneath him had control nearly slipping out of his hands.

He rolled with her, tugging away the spread she'd tangled around them, sinking with her into the pool of pillows. He dragged at her shorts, drawing them down, away, then toyed with the last barrier, the little swatch of blush-colored lace.

"Oh my." Her hips jerked and her vision blurred. "I can't—"

"You should be dancing through the woods under a full moon." He murmured it, delighting in her body, the shape of it, the glorious response of it to every touch. He traced a scatter of freckles on her quivering belly and smiled as he shaped a star. "Should've figured it."

Then he slid a finger under the lace.

Pressure slammed into her, a smothering weight of velvet that had her fighting for one gulp of air. Heat flashed with the shock of a fireball. Her eyes went blind, the stunned cry ripped from her throat, and the pressure burst into a flare of pleasure dark as moonless midnight.

She went limp with it, the hand that had gripped his shoulder sliding bonelessly to the tangled sheets.

So hot, he thought, and his hands weren't completely steady as he drew the lace down her legs. So wet. So beautifully ready. He felt his heart slamming in his chest as her heavy eyes flickered open and that clouded gold fixed on him.

"I've never…"

"I know." He was the first, and it made him mad to have her. "Again," he murmured, and brought her close, so desperately close that her hips arched up to meet him when he came into her.

His muscles screamed, his blood seemed to snarl as he met both heat and resistance. "Hold on." He panted it, linked his hands with hers.

She felt herself reaching again, flying toward that astonishing peak. The pain was a shock, so mixed with pleasure she couldn't separate the two. Then she was opening for him, taking him into her. Mating. And there was only pleasure.

Movement and magic combined to sweep her

off on some high, curving wave that crested so slowly, so gracefully that she seemed to tremble on its peak endlessly before sliding down, and down into a quiet and shimmering pool.

Resting there, with him on her, in her, she wrapped herself around him and sighed his name.

Chapter Nine

She could smell the heady and exotic fragrances of the tropical bouquet on her dresser. The sun poured through the windows and beat warmly against her face.

If she kept her eyes closed she could picture herself in some lush and deserted jungle, gloriously naked and tangled around her lover.

Her lover. What a marvelous phrase that was.

She let it repeat in her mind, over and over, as she turned her head to press her lips to his throat. But when he started to shift, she tightened her grip.

"Do you have to move?"

His mind didn't seem to want to clear. She was still inside it as completely as he was still inside her. "You're so little."

"I've been working out." She wanted to keep tasting it, the hot, dusky flavor of his throat. "I'm starting to get biceps."

He had to smile. He eased back just enough to pinch her upper arm where the tiny muscle melted like wax under his fingers. "Wow."

She laughed. "Okay. I'm *almost* getting biceps. In a few more weeks, nobody's going to call me Pencil-Arm."

"You don't have pencil arms," he murmured, distracted by the texture of her skin along her elbow. "They're slender. Smooth."

She studied his face, marveling at the concentration in his eyes as he traced his finger from her shoulder to her wrist. Did he have any idea just what that absent brush of fingers did inside her body? She didn't see how he could, or how he could possibly understand what it was like for her to look at that beautifully sculpted profile and know that for a little while he belonged to her.

Was it because she was in love with him that their lovemaking had taken on such a brilliant sheen? Was it because he was her first, her only, that she couldn't imagine being so close, so intimate with anyone else?

Whatever the reason, she would treasure what he'd given her. And she would hope she'd given him something he would remember in return.

"I have to ask." Her smile was a little apologetic. "I know it's probably pitifully typical, but…well, I need to know."

His gaze had come back to her face, and it was wary. He was afraid she would ask him how he felt, what he wanted, where this was leading. Since he was still struggling with the first part of that, he had no idea what followed.

"Was I—was it…" How did one phrase it? "Was it all right?" she asked him.

Then tension in his stomach dissolved. "Darcy." Struck by a wave of tenderness, he lowered his mouth and kissed her, long and deep. "What do you think?"

"I stopped being able to think." Her eyes opened slowly, glowed into his. "Everything got jumbled. I always imagined that I'd remember all the details, sort of step-by-step. But I couldn't pay attention. There was so much to feel."

"Sometimes…" He wanted her mouth again, and took it. "Thinking's overrated."

"Thoughts just slide out of my head when you do that." Her hands stroked down his back as she floated on the kiss. "And when you started to touch me, everything got so…hot."

He groaned against her mouth, then swallowed her gasp as he hardened inside her. "You don't have to pay attention," he told her. "Just let me have you."

Her breath came fast and thick, shattered on each long, slow stroke. She came on a moan and a shudder that ripped through him like claws. He gripped her hips, lifted them. "More. Give me more this time," he demanded, and drove deep, dragging her over the edge with him.

Later, when she was alone, she caught her reflection in the mirror over the bed. Her eyes went wide with shock at the image of herself, hair tousled, face glowing, her naked body sprawled over a tangle of sheets.

Could this be Darcy Wallace? The dutiful
daughter, the conscientious librarian, the shy and
pitiful doormat from Kansas?

She looked…ripe, she decided. Aware. And
oh, so satisfied. Then she bit her curving lip as she
wondered if she'd have the nerve to look up into
the mirror the next time Mac made love with her.

The next time.

Overcome with joy, she hugged a pillow and
rolled. He wanted her. She didn't care what the
reasons were, it was enough that he did. There
had been simmering promise in the kiss they'd
shared before he'd left her. He'd asked her to
have a late supper with him in his office.

He wanted her.

Was it so impossible to believe she could find
a way to make him keep wanting her? And to find
a way to turn that wanting into love?

Curling into the pillow, she rested her head. It
would be a gamble. She would be risking what
she had now in the hope for more. Because he'd
been right, she admitted. What he'd said in the
rooftop garden had been a bull's-eye. She did
want marriage and family and permanence. She

wanted children. She wanted, desperately, to be able to take this love that threatened to flood right out of her heart and give it.

And for once in her life, she wanted to feel loved in return. Not the lukewarm affection of duty, not the kindly indulgence of affection, but the hot-blooded and dangerous love that sprang from passion and lust and blind need.

The kind of love that could hurt, she thought, squeezing her eyes shut. The kind that lasted and grew and shot up and down the hills of the roller coaster and demanded screams of delight and terror.

She wanted it all. And she wanted it with Mac Blade.

How would she win his heart? She sighed a little, absently snuggling into the pillow as her limbs grew heavy. She would figure it out, she promised herself and sighed toward sleep.

After all, the only way to win was to play. And she was on a hot streak.

She wore the beaded jacket she'd fallen in love with on her first day at the hotel. Under it was a daring little excuse for a dress in lipstick red. The jacket gave her confidence, made her feel glamorous.

The dress made her feel just a bit sinful.

She wanted to try her hand at blackjack again, decided she might make it her signature game. If she was going to live in Vegas—and she was—and be involved with a man who ran a casino—which she hoped to be—she needed to be skilled in at least one form of gambling.

The slots, she decided, didn't take skill. She'd proved that herself. Roulette appeared to be a bit repetitive, and craps…well, it looked wonderfully exciting and rousing, but she just couldn't follow the action.

But the cards were self-explanatory, and they always came up in a different and intriguing order.

She wandered for a while, just enjoying the crush of people, the raucous sounds, the pulse of excitement. The tables were crowded tonight, and the cards moved, fast and sharp. She was toying with joining a game, and had talked herself into risking a hundred dollars for the night when Serena came up beside her.

"I'm glad to see you decided to get out for a while." Angling her head, Serena took in the glittery jacket. "Celebrating?"

"Um." Darcy felt color flood her face. She could hardly tell Mac's mother she was, in her way, celebrating making love to him. "I just wanted to dress up. I bought all these clothes and I've been living in slacks and shorts."

"I know just how you feel. Nothing perks up the soul like a great dress. And that's a great one."

"Thanks. You don't think it's too…red?"

"Absolutely not. So are you going to try your luck here?"

"I was thinking about it." She nibbled her lip. "I hate to join a table where everyone knows what they're doing. It must be irritating to have a novice plop down and slow the game."

"It's part of the game, and the luck of the draw. If you stick to the five- or ten-dollar tables, most people will be willing to help you out a bit."

"You were a dealer."

"Yes, I was. And a good one."

"Would you teach me?"

"To deal?"

"To play," Darcy stated. "And to win."

"Well…" Serena's smile spread slowly. "Go get us a table in the bar. I'll be along in a minute."

"Split your sevens."

Eyes sober, Darcy followed instructions, setting the two sevens she'd been dealt side by side on the silver table in the lounge. "And this is supposed to be good, right? Not stressful because now I have two hands to worry about."

Serena just grinned. "Cover your bet on the second hand." She dealt Darcy her next cards. "Three for ten on your first hand, six for thirteen on your second. Dealer has an eight showing, what do you do?"

"Okay." Darcy wiped her damp palms on her knees. "I double down on the first hand, then take a hit." Remembering the ritual she'd been taught, she counted out the bar nuts standing in the place of chips, then tapped a finger on her cards. "A three—thirteen. I have to take another one."

"Pulled a six for nineteen. Holding on nineteen?"

"Yeah. Now we do this one." She tapped her

finger on the second hand and winced at the steely eyes of the king she drew. "Well, at least that was fast."

"Busted on twenty-three." Serena raked in the nuts, and cards, then turned over her down card. "Dealer has eleven, fourteen, and breaks on twenty-four."

"So I win on the first hand, but I doubled the bet so it's like winning twice. That's good."

"You're getting it. Now if you want to buck the house, you let that bet ride on the next hand."

Darcy stared down at her pile of nuts. "It's a lot—twenty nuts on one hand."

"Two thousand." Serena twinkled at her. "Didn't I mention the nuts are a hundred a pop?"

"Good God, I've eaten a dozen. Let's go for it."

"Is this game open, ladies?"

Serena tipped up her face for her husband's kiss. "You got a stake, pal, you got a chair."

He snagged a bowl of pretzels from a neighboring table. "I think I can afford a few hands."

"Thousand-dollar chips. We got us a high roller." Delighted with the game, Serena rubbed her hands together. "Place your bets."

When Mac found them a half hour later, Darcy was sitting hip to hip with his father and giggling as she piled a mix of nuts and pretzels into a sloppy mountain on the table. "You're not supposed to hit on seventeen when the dealer's showing a two," Darcy said, sniffing experimentally at the smoke from Justin's slim cigar. "Why did you?"

"He's a card counter." Mac pulled up a chair and sat between his parents, eyeing his father. "We don't like card counters around here. We ask them politely to take their money elsewhere."

"I taught you how to count cards before you could handle a two-wheeler."

"Yeah." Mac's grin flashed and spread. "That's why I can spot 'em."

"Your father's still as slick as he was when he bet me a walk on the deck of the ship on one hand of twenty-one. He hit on seventeen then, too."

"Oh." Darcy's heart sighed. "That's so romantic."

"Serena didn't think so at the time." Justin sent Serena a long, slow smile. "But I changed her mind."

"I thought you were arrogant, dangerous and cocky. I still do," Serena added, sipping at her wine. "I just learned to like it."

"Are you two going to flirt with each other or play cards?" Mac demanded.

"They can do both," Darcy told him. "I've been watching."

"Learned anything?"

It was the delivery, smooth as silk, that flustered her as much as the words. She looked at him, large eyes shuttered by dark lashes. "If you don't bet, you don't win."

"I've got a couple hours off." He spoke to the table at large, but his eyes were on Darcy's as he rose, held out a hand. "I'll see you tomorrow," he said to his parents, then drew Darcy to her feet. "Let's go out."

"Out?"

"There's more to Vegas than The Comanche."

"Good night," she called over her shoulder as Mac was already pulling her away.

Justin drew on his cigar, tapped it idly. "The boy's a goner," he decided.

The minute she stepped outside, Darcy realized

she hadn't been out of the hotel after sunset since she arrived. For a moment she simply stood, between the tumbling sapphire water of a fountain and the grand gilded statue of the war chief.

The lights were dazzling, the traffic edgy. Vegas was a woman, she thought, part honky-tonk, part siren, bold, brassy and seductive.

"It's so…much," she decided.

"And there's always more. The Strip's a few blocks long, a few blocks wide, but you can smell money in every foot of it. Gambling's the core, but it's not a one-factory town anymore. Headliners, circus acts, wedding bells and rides for the kids."

He glanced back at the wide and towering double arch that was The Comanche. "We added a thousand rooms five years ago. We could add a thousand more and still fill them."

"It's a huge responsibility. Running an enterprise of this size."

"I like it."

"The challenge?" she wondered. "Or the power, or the excitement?"

"All of it." He turned back, then taking her hand stepped back. He hadn't gotten beyond her face in the bar. Those eyes of hers always seemed to capture his mind first. Now he took in the glittering glamour of her jacket and the invitational red of her dress.

"I should have stolen more than a couple hours. You need to be taken out on the town."

"I'd love a couple of hours. Where should we go?"

"I can't manage a drive into the mountains in the moonlight, but I can take you for a walk through a tunnel full of fantasies."

He took her walking on Freemont, where the street was covered and full of lights. Colors circled and bled overhead, and the ever present clack of the slots added a musical, carnival feel. She could marvel at the light show, delight in the music and walked hand in hand with him on what was so suddenly and unexpectedly an innocent date.

He bought her ice cream, and made her laugh.

She rode the elevator to the top of The Stratosphere with him, thrilled at the idea that she was rising up inside of that towering needle that stood at the edge of the Strip. And though she stared then gulped at the sight of the rooftop roller coaster, the silent challenge in his eyes had her scooting into the car with him.

"I've never ridden a roller coaster in my life."

"You might as well start with a champ," he told her.

"I tried a Tilt-A-Whirl once at a carnival but…" She trailed off. "Are you sure this is safe?"

"Almost everyone who gets on gets off again. The odds are good." He laughed at the horrified look in her eyes, then took advantage—as he'd intended to—when the coaster started its climb and she gripped him in a death hold. "I want to kiss you."

"Okay, but you could have done that on the ground." She lifted her face, which she'd buried in his shoulder.

"Not yet," he murmured, but laid his hands on her cheeks. "Not quite yet."

Lulled, she smiled and her heart began to beat normally again. "It's not so bad. I didn't realize it would be so nice and slow."

Then they dipped, spinning fast into a free fall that shot her stomach hard against her ribs and burned white-hot fear into her throat.

"Now." And he took her mouth greedily as they swung over the edge of the world.

She couldn't breathe. There wasn't even breath to scream. They were flying, rocketing up, plunging down, shoved into the void then snatched back while his mouth assaulted hers with a single-minded intensity that left her stupefied.

Speed, light, screams. And that firestorm of stunning heat that refused to be stopped. Dizzy, breathless, helplessly caught in the crosshatch of arousal and fear, she clung to him.

And gave him what he'd wanted—crazed, half-terrified surrender.

Her head was still reeling after they'd jerked to a stop. Her fingers continued to grip his jacket, as if fused there. "God." The word exploded from her lips. "I've never felt anything like that before. She shuddered once. "Can we do it again?"

His grin flashed. "Oh yeah."

She felt drunk and giddy by the time they stood on the street again. "Oh, that was wonderful. It made my head spin." She laughed as he slipped a supporting arm around her waist. "I won't be able to walk a straight line for hours."

"Then you'll have to lean on me—which was part of my plan."

Laughing again, she threw back her head to watch an explosion of fireworks. Jewel colors shot into the black sky, and fountained there. "Everything's so bright here, so bold. Nothing's too high or too big or too fast." She turned into him. "Nothing's impossible here."

Wrapping her arms around his neck, she kissed him with a passion that had waited a long time to wake. "I want to do everything. I want to do everything twice, then pick the best and do it again."

He slid his arms under her jacket and discovered to his delight that the dress left her back bare to his hands. "We've got a little time before I have to get back. What would you like to do?"

"Well…" Her eyes sparkled in the neon. "I've never seen an exotic dancer."

"And your second choice would be?"

"I just wonder what it would be like in one of those places where the women dance topless and slide around on those poles."

"No, I'm definitely not taking you to a strip joint."

"I've seen naked women before."

"No."

"All right." She moved a shoulder, began to walk casually beside him. "I'll just go by myself some other time."

He shot her a look, narrowed his eyes, but she only smiled up sunnily. He considered himself highly skilled at judging a bluff. And knew when he was up against a better hand.

"Ten minutes," he muttered. "And you don't say a word while we're inside."

"Ten minutes is fine." Delighted with the victory, she tucked her arm through his.

"The patriotic one was double-jointed, I'm sure of it." With another fascinating experience under her belt, Darcy breezed into Mac's office just ahead of him. "The one with the little flag over her—"

"I know the one you mean." Every time he thought he had her pegged, Mac thought, she flustered him. She hadn't been the least bit embarrassed or shocked. Instead she'd been fascinated.

"The way they slid around on that pole, they

must practice for hours. And the muscle control, it's phenomenal."

"I can't believe I let you talk me into taking you into a place like that."

"I had no idea."

"Obviously."

"No, I mean about you." She sat on the arm of a chair. He was already behind his desk, scanning the screens.

"What about me?"

"That under that suave, sophisticated exterior, you're really a fuddy-duddy at heart."

He stared at her, unsure if he should be amused or insulted. "Anyone who uses the expression 'fuddy-duddy' in a sentence automatically assumes fuddy-duddy status."

"I never heard that."

"It's written down somewhere. Are you hungry?"

"Not really." She couldn't sit still and rose to circle the room. "I had such a wonderful time. It's been the most incredible day of my life—and I've had some incredible days lately. Everything's churning about inside me." She wrapped her arms around herself as if to hold it all in. "I don't think there's any room for food."

Her jacket caught the lights as she moved, glittering like jewel-toned stars that reminded him of the fireworks. But it was her face—it always seemed to be her face—that held his attention. "Champagne?"

She laughed, a warm delighted sound. "There's always room for champagne. Imagine me being able to say that. It's like every minute I'm here is another little miracle."

He took a bottle from the small refrigerator behind the wet bar, watching her as he opened it. She was glowing, he thought, eyes, cheeks, lips. Everything about her seemed to pulse with energy and fresh, unshadowed joy.

Seeing it, feeling it, aroused, contented and unnerved him. Be with me, she'd asked him. And being with her, on a walk down a crowded street, alone in a tumbled bed, over a candlelit table, was becoming uncomfortably vital.

But she was glowing. How could he take his eyes off her? "I like seeing you happy."

"Then you must be having a good night, too.

I've never been so happy." She took the glass he offered, twirling around as she sipped. "Can I stay here with you awhile, watch the people?"

Did she really have no idea how she affected him? he wondered. "Stay as long as you want."

"Will you tell me what you're looking for when you watch the screens? I don't see anything but people."

"Trouble, scams, tells."

"What are tells?"

"Everybody has them. Gestures, repetitive habits that tell you what's going on in the head." He smiled at her. "You link your fingers together when you're nervous. It keeps you from biting your nails. You cock your head to the left when you're concentrating."

"Oh. Like the way you put your hands in your pockets when you're frustrated—so you don't punch someone."

He lifted a brow. "Good."

"It's easy when you're watching a handful of people, but there are so many," she added, gesturing to the screens. "How do you pick them out?"

"You get to know what to look for. This is only

backup. The first line of defense against scam artists is the dealer." He walked up behind her, laid a hand on her shoulder so they could watch the screens together. "Then the floor man, the pit boss, the shift boss. And over it all is the eye in the sky."

"This?"

"No, this is a wink. We have a control room with hundreds of screens like this. The staff in there watches the casino from every angle, and they're linked to the floor men, the shift and pit bosses with radios. They'll spot a hand mucker—"

"A what?"

"Card palming. The scam artist is dealt say a six and an eight, he palms them, and switches them with a queen and ace for a blackjack. Cheating's a problem—more now than it used to be when you were dealing with loaded dice and fast hands. We're talking body computers these days."

Body computers, she thought, scam artist. Hand mucking. Wouldn't that be a fascinating backdrop for a book? "What do you do when you catch someone cheating?"

"Show them the door."

"That's it?"

"They don't walk out with our money."

The chill in his voice had Darcy glancing back at his face. "I bet they don't," she murmured.

"We run a clean room, the cameras there and in all the counting areas help keep it honest. But the house always has the edge. It's not hard to win money in The Comanche, but odds are, you won't keep it."

"Because you want to keep playing." She understood that. It was so hard to stop when there was a chance for more.

"And the longer you play, the more you'll put back."

"But it's worth it, isn't it? If you've enjoyed yourself. If it's made you happy."

"As long as you know what you're risking." He brought her to her feet, and saw that she understood they were no longer talking about table games and slots.

"The danger's part of the allure." Her heart began to thud as he took the glass from her hand and set it aside. "That, and the whiff of sin. You get a taste for it."

"And why stop at a bite or two, when you can have all you want." His gaze roamed over her face, lingering on her mouth, then sliding down. "Take off your jacket."

"We're in your office."

His eyes came back to hers, and his smile was slow and dangerous. "I wanted you, here, the first day you came in. Now I'm going to have you, here. Take off your jacket."

Mesmerized, she slipped it off, let it fall in a colorful pool over the arm of the chair. When she realized she'd linked her fingers together, she pulled them apart. And made him smile again.

"I don't mind you being nervous. I like it. It's exciting to know you're a little afraid, but when I touch you, you'll give." He reached out to toy with the sassy red strap on her shoulder. The dress clung to every quiet curve. "What've you got on under there, Darcy?"

Her breath shuddered out. "Hardly anything."

His eyes flashed, a clash of swords in the sun. "I don't want to be gentle this time. Will you risk it?"

She nodded, would have spoken, but he was already dragging her against him. His mouth was bruising and hungry and tasted of such raw passion she could only marvel he felt it for her.

Then he was pulling her to the floor, and the shock of that alone had her gasping. His hands took her over, body and mind, racing over her, taking, possessing, inciting a fury of sensations.

All she could think was that it was like the roller coaster, a fast and reckless ride. Glorying in it, she yanked desperately at his jacket, tugged at his shirt while the pulse pounding in her seemed to scream hurry, hurry, hurry.

She moaned as he peeled the dress down, and the sound raged through his blood. Her breasts were small and firm and when he filled his mouth with the taste of them she fisted her hands in his hair, urging him to take more. Desperate for the taste of flesh, her flesh, he used tongue and teeth until she writhed under him, her sobbing breaths like a drumbeat to his greed.

But still it wasn't enough.

His mouth streaked down, laying a line of heat on skin that had gone hot and damp. Her muscles quivered beneath his tongue, her body shivered under his busy, relentless hands. His own breath was ragged when he gripped her restless hips and lifted them.

The fast plunge ripped a scream from her throat. The fire that shot through her was molten, shocking her system with sensations so acute she feared for a moment they would simply tear her apart. The climax rushed through her, a towering wave of hot, hard pleasure that tossed her high, sucked her deep. Helpless, she tossed an arm over her eyes and let it drag her where it would.

When she thought there could be no more, he pulled her mercilessly over the next edge.

She lay bonelessly as he yanked off the rest of his clothes. Her skin glowed under the lights, flushed and damp. Her mouth was swollen from his. When he drew her up, her head fell weakly back, leaving him no choice but to plunder her soft mouth.

"Stay with me." He murmured it as he assaulted her neck, her shoulders. He shifted, bringing her over him, brought her down until she took him into her, closed that glorious heat around him.

Her moan was long and deep and broken. He

watched as flickers of fresh pleasure moved over her face and into the clouded eyes that opened and fixed on his.

"Take what you want." His hands moved up her body and covered her breasts.

She was already moving. Her body was unable to rest. There was a shock of control, of power, a nervy kind of energy that demanded movement. Tantalizing. She arched back and drove herself mad.

Everything inside her was as bright, as brilliant, as reckless and bold as the world she now lived in. A world where nothing was too big or too fast, or too much.

He was quivering beneath her, and his hands were rough as they gripped her hips. A new thrill snaked through her, the knowing that she was taking him with her.

Stay with me, he'd demanded. And she wanted nothing more than to obey.

When the climax bowed her back, when it had her melting down on him, he rolled her over, his body plunging, his heart pounding, until both body and heart emptied themselves into her.

Chapter Ten

The phone woke Darcy at five past nine. She thought blearily that her days of working an ordinary eight-hour day were over. It had been nearly four in the morning when she'd given in to exhaustion. And even then she'd been wrapped around Mac.

Since she was alone in the big bed, she had to assume he'd figured out a way to function on little to no sleep. If he could learn, so could she.

She yawned widely, reached for the phone with her eyes still hopefully shut. "Hello?" she mumbled, and buried both her head and receiver in the pillow.

Fifteen minutes later she was sitting straight up in bed, staring at nothing. Maybe she'd been dreaming, she thought, and stared at the phone. Had she actually just talked to an editor in New York? Had that editor actually asked to see her work?

She pressed a hand to her heart. It was beating, fast but steady. She could feel the light chill from the air-conditioning on her bare shoulders. She was wide-awake.

Not a dream, she told herself, bringing her knees up and wrapping her arms tightly around them. Not a dream at all.

Her story was all over the media—the editor had said as much. Darcy had told reporters that she was writing a book, and now the next miracle had happened. A publisher wanted to see it.

It was only because of the attention from the press, Darcy thought, resting her forehead on her knees. She was an oddity, a story in herself, and the publisher would consider her manuscript because of the public's interest in the writer, and not the work.

And that, she thought with a sigh, didn't make her a writer.

What difference did it make? She sat straight again, balling her fists. It was a foot in the door, wasn't it? A chance to see if—no, not to see, she corrected, to *prove* her work had merit.

She'd send the first book in, and the opening chapters of the second. She would let them stand or fall on their own.

Tossing the sheets aside, she scrambled out of bed, bundled into a robe and raced downstairs to turn those first two chapters into gems.

She said nothing to Mac, to anyone, afraid she would jinx herself. Superstition was another new character trait, or perhaps one she'd kept buried. She worked steadily through the day, ruthlessly cutting, lovingly polishing her words until she was forced to admit she could do no better.

While the pages printed out, she retrieved her list of agents. If she intended to be a professional, she told herself, then she would need professional representation. It was time to take the big risk. Finally take it.

They were just names to her, faceless power symbols. How would she know which one to pick, which one would see something inside her worthy of their time and attention?

The face of the slot had been only stars and moons, she remembered. She'd gambled everything once. It wasn't so hard to do it again. Following impulse, she shut her eyes, circled her finger in the air, then jabbed it onto the list.

"Let's see how lucky you are," Darcy murmured, and calculating she had fifteen minutes before offices closed on the East Coast, picked up the phone.

Twenty minutes later she had representation, or at least the promise to read the manuscript and sample of her work, and to negotiate if the publisher made an offer.

More than satisfied, Darcy typed up a cover letter, then called the desk to request an overnight bag and form before she could change her mind.

She nearly did so while the bellman waited for her to seal the envelope. She very nearly gave in to the dozens of excuses whirling in her head.

It wasn't ready. She wasn't ready. The book needed more work. She needed more time. She was sending work she'd slaved over to strangers. She should ask someone's advice before she mailed the pages. She should call the agent back and tell her she wanted to finish the second manuscript rather than submitting the first.

Coward, she berated herself and, setting her jaw, handed the bellman the envelope. "Will this go out today?"

"Yes, ma'am. It'll be in—" he glanced at the address on the form "—New York tomorrow morning."

"Tomorrow." She felt the blood drain out of her face. "Good. Thank you." She handed him some crumpled bills as a tip, then sat down the minute he was gone and dropped her head between her knees.

It was done. There was no going back now. In a matter of days she would know if she was good enough. Finally good enough. And if she wasn't...

She simply couldn't face failing at this. Not this. As long as she could remember, she'd wanted this one thing. Had set it aside time after time after time. Now there was no one to tell her to be practical, to accept her own limitations. There were no more excuses.

Steadier, she sat up, took two long breaths. She'd plugged in her stake, she told herself, and she'd pulled the lever. Now she would have to wait for the end of the spin.

When the phone rang, she stared at it, horrified. It was the editor calling back, she thought frantically, telling her there had been a mistake.

Holding her breath, she picked up the phone. "Hello," she said, with her eyes tightly shut.

"Hello yourself, little girl."

"Daniel." His name came out on something close to a sob.

"Aye. Is something wrong, lass?"

"No, no." She pressed a hand to her face and let out a quick, nervous laugh. "Everything's fine. Wonderful. How are you?"

"Right as rain." The way his voice boomed through the receiver seemed to prove it. "I thought I should let you know, I lost every penny in a leveraged buyout."

"I—I—" She blinked so rapidly the room spun in front of her eyes. "All of it?"

His laughter roared out, forcing her to pull the receiver several inches away from her ear. "Just joking with you, lass."

"Oh." She pressed a hand to her speeding heart. "Ha-ha."

"Got your blood moving, didn't it? I'm just calling to let you know we made some money already."

"Made some? Already?"

"You know, Darcy girl, you're using the same tone for the good news as you did for the bad. That's a good sign of a steady nerve."

"I don't feel steady," she admitted. "But I feel lots of nerves."

"You'll do. We made a tidy little sum on a short-term deal, an in and out sort of thing. You should go buy yourself a bauble."

She moistened her lips. "How big a bauble?"

He laughed again. "That's my girl. We pulled in a quick fifty, just getting our feet wet."

"I can get some nice earrings for fifty dollars."

"Fifty thousand."

"Thousand," she repeated though her tongue seemed to tangle on the word. "Are you joking again?"

"Buy the bauble," he told her. "Making money's a fine way to pass the time, but enjoying it's better. Now tell me when you're coming to see me. My Anna wants to meet you."

"I may be coming East—on business—in the next few weeks."

"That's fine then. You plan to come here, spend some time, meet the rest of the family, or those I can gather up. Children scatter on you. It's a crime. My wife pines for them."

"I will come. I miss you."

"You've a sweet heart, Darcy."

"Daniel…do you…" It had to be delicately put, she thought, but it had to be put. "Mac mentioned, that is, he seemed to think you might have the idea that we'd suit each other. That you were, well, planting seeds along those lines."

"Planting seeds, is it! Planting seeds. Ha! The boy needs a cuff on the ear. Did I say a word? I ask you."

"Well, not exactly, but—"

"Where do they get this idea that I'm scheming behind their backs? I didn't drop you into his lap, did I?"

"No, but—"

"Not that it doesn't take a push to get these young people to do their duty—and to see what's best for them. Dawdle around is what they do. My wife deserves babies to bounce on her knees in her twilight years, doesn't she?"

"Yes, of course. It's just that—"

"Damn right I do—she does," he corrected quickly. "Boy's going to be thirty in another month or so, and is he settling down to make a family? He is not," Daniel rolled on before Darcy could speak. "And what's so wrong with giving him a bit of a nudge, I'd like to know, if you suit him?"

"Do I?" she murmured. "Do I suit him?"

"I'm saying so, and who'd know better?" He huffed, then his voice shifted, became sly and persuasive. "He's a good-looking young man, don't you think?"

"Yes, I do."

"Strong stock, a good brain. There's a kind heart in him, too, and a fine sense of responsibility. He's a steady one, stands for his friends and his family. A woman couldn't do better than my Robbie."

"No, I don't see how she could."

"We're not talking about she," Daniel said with some impatience. "We're talking about you. You've got a spark for him now, don't you, Darcy girl?"

She thought of the fireworks exploding over the city the night before. Her spark for Mac was every bit as huge and bright and volatile. "Daniel, I'm so desperately in love with him."

"Well now."

"Please." She winced at the booming pleasure in his voice. "I'm trusting you with that because I need to tell someone."

"Why aren't you telling him?"

"Because I don't want to scare him off." There, she'd said it, she thought, biting her lip. It was no more than a plot.

"So…you're giving him some time to woo you, and come around to thinking it was his idea."

Now she winced. "It's not really that devious. It's just—"

"What the devil's wrong with devious? Devious gets the job done, doesn't it?"

"I suppose." Her lips trembled into a smile. How could she help it? "He cares for me, I know he does, but I think part of it comes from that fine sense of responsibility. I'm willing to wait until he doesn't feel responsible."

"Don't wait too long."

"I'm hoping I won't have to." She smiled. "I have some ideas."

She wasn't in the market for a bauble, but she rented a car. Buying one was going to wait until she could decide if the sports car or the sedan suited her new and developing life-style.

She secretly hoped it would be the sports car.

Armed with maps, she began the task of familiarizing herself with the city, the one beyond the Strip. She cruised downtown, noting the huge building cranes that loomed like giant, hovering birds. Growth was everywhere, from the spectacular hotel resorts, to the developments that sprawled into the desert.

She parked and walked the malls, the grocery

store and drugstores, giving herself a chance to observe the life that pulsed here beyond the casinos.

She saw children playing in yards, houses tucked side by side in neighborhoods. She saw schools and churches, quiet streets and crowded ones. She saw sprawling homes that faced the eerie peace of the desert and the tumble of rocks that made the mountains beyond.

She saw a life she could begin to build.

Circling back, she found a library and went inside to gather more information on the place she would make her home.

It was after seven when she got back to her suite, pleasantly tired and more than eager to put her aching feet up. She was certain she'd walked twenty miles. Though she hadn't bought a bauble, she had made an appointment to view a property the following day.

She thought she might become a home owner very soon.

"There you are." Mac stepped up to the elevator the moment the doors opened. "I was getting worried."

"I'm sorry. I was out exploring." She tossed her purse aside and started to smile, but her mouth was soon busy against his.

He knew the sense of relief was out of proportion, as was the irritation he'd felt when he hadn't been able to find her anywhere in the hotel. "You shouldn't have gone out alone. You don't know your way around."

Responsibility, she thought, and wanted to sigh. "I got a map. I thought it was time I saw a little more of the city."

She started to tell him about the house she planned to see the next day, then held her tongue. The news was hers for now, she thought, just as the call from New York was hers.

"You spent some time in the sun." He ran a fingertip down her nose and made her wrinkle it.

"I'll have to remember to get a hat before I turn into one big freckle. The air's so hot and dry. It must be murder on the skin, but I really love it."

"It's easy to get dehydrated."

"Mmm. You're right." She walked over to take a bottle of water from behind the bar. "I saw people with water bottles hooked on their belts.

Like hikers or explorers, and so much building going on. Men in hard hats working a hundred, two hundred feet in the air. Slot machines in the grocery store."

"You went to a grocery store."

"I wanted to see what it was like," she said, evading. "All this boom in the downtown area, then suddenly, you're in a quiet suburban neighborhood, with kids and dogs in the yard, and it all seems so cozily settled."

"I'd have taken you around if I'd known you wanted to go."

"I knew you were busy."

"I'm not busy now. My parents booted me out, with orders to take the night off."

A smile curved her lips. "I really love your parents."

"So do I. Come for a drive with me." He held out a hand. "We'll find some moonlight."

In the distance, Vegas shimmered like a mirage. The floor of the desert stretched in every direction, barely marred by the slice of road. Overhead the sky was a clear, dark sea, studded by countless stars and graced by the floating ball of a white moon.

In the distant hills a coyote called, and the plaintive sound carried like a bell on the air that had cooled with moonrise.

He'd put the top down so that she could lay her head back and let starlight shower on her face. Wind danced lightly across the sand as they sat in silence.

"You forget this exists when you're in there." She looked toward the colors and shapes of the city. "The West, wild and dangerous and beautiful."

"A long way from Kansas." It was too easy to picture her there, away from the arid wind, the gaudy lights. "Do you miss the green? The fields?"

"No." She didn't have to think about it. "There's something so powerful in the siennas and soft reds, the baked-out greens and browns of this land. But you didn't grow up here, either." She turned her head to look at him. "You lived back East, didn't you?"

"The house is in New Jersey, just outside of Atlantic City. My parents didn't want to raise a family in hotel rooms over a casino. But we spent plenty of time there. Duncan and I used to hunker down in the security bay over the tables. Before everything was electronic, that's where they watched the room. My mother would have skinned me if she knew I'd taken him up there."

"Rightfully so. It must have been dangerous."

"Part of the appeal, right?" His grin flashed and to her secret joy he began to play absently with her hair. "There's a story about the night one of the men fell out and landed facedown on a craps table."

"Ow! Was he hurt? What happened?"

"Rumor persists that some guy bet five dollars on his ass. The game doesn't stop for much."

She chuckled and settled her head on his shoulder. "It was exciting for you, being a part of all of that. Why did you choose to work here and not back East?"

"There's only one Vegas. No point in settling for less than the best."

Her heart gave a little jerk at the sentiment, spoken with such casual confidence. But she ignored it. "Is the rest of your family involved with the casinos?"

"Duncan's managing the riverboat. It suits him down to the ground, cruising along the Mississippi and charming the ladies."

"You're close?"

"Yeah. We are, all of us. Geography doesn't change that. Gwen's a doctor, lives in Boston— as do several assorted cousins. She had a baby a few months ago."

"Boy or girl?"

"A girl. Anna, after my grandmother. I have two or three hundred pictures," he added with a smile, "if you'd like to see her."

"I'd love to. You have another sister, the youngest?"

"Mel. She's a live wire. The eyes of an angel and the right hook of a middleweight."

"I imagine she needed both," Darcy said dryly. "You probably teased her unmercifully."

"No more than was my right and duty. Besides, I'm the one who taught her how to punch. No girlie little slaps for my baby sister."

"I bet they're all beautiful. With heart-stopping faces and killer smiles." She turned her head, let herself trace his mouth with her fingertip. "And between the looks and the breeding, they're a confident bunch. The kind who walk into a room, take one slow glance around and know exactly where they stand. I always envied that innate sense of self."

"I thought the word was *arrogance*."

"It is, but it's not always a criticism. Did you argue all the time?"

"As often as humanly possible."

"No one argued in my house. They reasoned. At least in an argument you have a chance to win."

"I've noticed you hold your own in that area."

"Beginner's luck," she claimed. "Wait until I'm seasoned a bit. I'll be a terror." She grinned. "Then I'll learn how to punch, in case arguing doesn't work."

Her lips were still curved when his lowered to them. The easy kiss turned dark quickly, began to heat rapidly around the edges. They both shifted, moving into it, into each other.

Emotion surged through him so powerfully, so violently that fury sprang up to tangle with need. "I shouldn't want you this much." He dragged her head back to try to clear his own. But all he could see were those dark gold eyes, and what was the shadow of himself drowning in them. "It's too damn much."

She remembered his words of the night before and gave them back to him. "Take what you need."

"I've been trying to. It doesn't stop."

The words sent a wild thrill soaring through her. Recklessly she knelt on the seat beside him, watched his gaze lower and follow the movement of her fingers as she unbuttoned her blouse. "Try again," she murmured.

He should never have touched her, was all he could think, because now he couldn't seem to stop. He drove the long, straight road back to Vegas at a fast clip, with Darcy sleeping like a child beside him, her head on his shoulder.

He'd taken her in the front seat of the car like a hormone-rattled teenager. He'd driven himself into her with a blind desperation, as though his life had depended on it.

And Lord help him, he wanted to do it again.

He'd broken all the rules with her. A man who made his living with games knew the rules, and when they could and should be ignored. He'd had no right to ignore them with her.

She'd been innocent and alone, and had trusted him.

He'd let his needs, and hers, step ahead of that. Now he was so tangled up in her, in what he wanted, in what was right, that nothing was clear.

He was going to have to step back. There was no question of it. She needed room, and the chance to test those wings of hers. No one had ever given her that chance, including himself.

He could keep her, he knew it. She thought she loved him, and he could make her go on thinking it. Until eventually, he thought with an inner lurch, that glow of hers began to fade against the neon and glitter, and that light of fascinated joy dulled in her eyes.

Keeping her would ruin her, change her and eventually break her. That was one gamble he wouldn't take.

Caring for her left him only one answer. He had to back away and give her a nudge in the opposite direction. In the direction that was right for her.

He should do it quickly for her sake, and yes, for his own.

She was the only woman who'd ever slipped uninvited into his mind at odd hours of the day and night. He wanted to resent it but found that he was already afraid of the time that would come when she would fade into a memory.

And he was already furious thinking of the time when he would become little more than that to her.

She'd think of him now and then, he reflected, when she was tucked into some pretty home in a green-lawned suburbia. Children playing at her feet, a dog sleeping in the yard and a husband who wouldn't appreciate the magic of her nearly enough on his way home for dinner.

It was exactly where she belonged, exactly where she would go once he worked up the courage to cut the ties that bound her to him. Ties of gratitude, excitement and sex, he thought and despised himself for wanting to hold her with them.

He'd spoken no less than the truth when he'd told her she didn't belong in the world he lived in. He believed that absolutely. She would come to the same truth once the gloss had dulled a bit.

Virtue and sin didn't mate comfortably.

He glanced down as he drove along the Strip and watched the carnival lights from the neon splash over her face. He would have to let her go, he told himself. But not yet.

Not quite yet.

Chapter Eleven

The house grew up out of the sand like a little castle fashioned of soft colors and magic shapes. Darcy's first sight of it shot an arrow of love and longing into her heart.

It was tucked among palms, and desert plants were scattered near the wide sunny deck. The soft red of the tile roof accented the cool ivory and buffed browns of the exterior. The multi-levels gave it a variety of charming rooflines and made her think of artistically placed building blocks.

It had a tower, a canny little spear that had her romantic heart picturing princesses and knights, even while the practical part of her nature snagged it greedily as the perfect writing space.

It was already hers, even before she stepped inside. She barely heard the realtor's professional chatter.

Only three years old. Custom-built. The family moved back East. It's just come on the market. Bound to be a quick mover.

"Hmm." Darcy responded simply as they started up the brick walkway to the door flanked by glass etched with stars.

Stars had been lucky for her, she thought.

She stepped into the entrance onto the sand-colored tiles, let her gaze travel up to the lofty ceiling. Skylights. Perfect. It was an airy space with walls painted a cool, soft yellow. She would leave them alone, she decided, listening to her heels click on the tile as she wandered.

Another deck stretched along the back, accessed by atrium doors in a quiet blond wood. No dark colors here, she thought. Everything would be light, fresh. Her eyes gleamed with pleasure as she looked beyond the deck to the sparkling waters of the swimming pool.

She let the realtor expound on the wonders of the kitchen, the subzero refrigerator, the custom-made cabinets, the granite counters. And was charmed by the cozy breakfast area tucked into a bay window. That was for family, she thought. For lazy Sunday mornings, and rushed school days, for quiet, late nights and cups of tea.

She would enjoy cooking here, she thought, studying the range, the double ovens, the mirror black cooktop. She'd always been a plain and pedestrian cook, but she thought she would like experimenting with recipes, with herbs, sauces.

The maid's room and laundry area off the kitchen were easily as big as her entire apartment in Kansas. Darcy didn't miss the irony, or the wonder of it.

She'd put a trestle table in the dining room, she mused. That would suit the tone and go well with the small tiled fireplace for chilly desert nights. Watercolors for the walls, soft bleeding tones.

She'd learn how to entertain, have intimate, casual dinner parties as well as sparkling, sophisticated ones. Loud, bawdy, backyard barbecues. Yes, she thought she could be a good, and what was better, an interesting hostess.

She toured each of the four bedrooms, checking views, space, approving the builder's choice of random-width pine for the floors, and the bright jazz of contrast tiles scattered in amusing patterns among the neutral colors of the baths.

She knew she goggled at the master suite, and didn't care. The two-level area boasted its own private deck, fireplace, an enormous dressing area with closets large enough to live in and a bath that rivaled the one at The Comanche with a lagoon-sized motorized tub in an unexpected clay color.

The treated skylight above it cut the glare while offering a dazzling view of desert blue sky.

Ferns, she imagined, in copper and brass pots, crowded together, all lush and green. She would jumble them on the wide ledge behind the tub and every bath would be like swimming in a secluded oasis.

The tower was octagon shaped, generous with windows. The walls were cream, the floor tiles the color of stone. Her work station would go there, she decided, facing the desert. Not a desk, but a long counter, perhaps in a sharp, deep blue for contrast. It would have dozens of drawers and cubbyholes.

She needed to go shopping for a computer system—a fax, a desktop copier. Reams of papers, she thought with a giddy burst of joy.

She would put a love seat on the other side of the room and create a small seating area, and she'd want shelves there, floor to ceiling, for books and small treasures.

She would sit there, writing hour after hour, and know she was a part of everything around her.

The realtor had been silent for the past several minutes. She'd been in the game long enough to know when to sell, and when to step back. The potential buyer didn't have much of a poker face, she mused, already imagining the tidy commission.

"It's a lovely property," the realtor said now. "A quiet, settled neighborhood, convenient for shopping but tucked just far away enough from the city to offer a sense of solitude." She offered Darcy a bright smile. "So, what do you think?"

Darcy pulled herself back and focused on the woman. "I'm so sorry, I've forgotten your name."

"It's Marion. Marion Baines."

"Oh, yes, Ms. Baines—"

"Marion."

"Marion. I appreciate you taking the time to show me through."

"Happy to do it." But she felt a little hitch in her stomach, a sign of a sale slipping away. "It might feel a little large for your needs. You did say you were single."

"Yes, I'm single."

"It might seem a bit overwhelming, but empty houses often do. You'd be amazed how it all comes together when it's furnished."

Darcy had already seen it come together as she could picture it furnished, perfectly, in her mind. "I'll take it."

"Oh." Marion's smile faltered, then spread. "Wonderful. I'm so pleased you want to make an offer. If you like we can use the kitchen to fill out the paperwork, and I can present your offer to the sellers this afternoon."

"I said I'd take it. I'll pay the asking price."

"You—well." Something in that fresh face and youthful eyes had her hesitating. Even as she ordered herself to keep her mouth shut and close the deal, she found herself speaking. "Ms. Wallace, Darcy…I'm contracted to represent the sellers, but I realize this is the first time you've bought property. I feel obligated to mention that it's usual to make an offer of…somewhat less than the asking price. The sellers may accept it, or counter."

"Yes, I know. But why shouldn't they get what they want?" She smiled and turned back to gaze out the window. "I'm going to."

It was so simple really, she discovered. A few forms to be filled out, papers to be signed, a check to be written. Earnest money, it was called. Darcy liked the sound of it. She was very earnest about the house.

She listened as home loans were explained to her, fixed interest rates, balloon payments, mortgage insurance. Then decided to keep it simple and pay cash.

When the settlement date was set, she breezed

out to her rented car, thrilled by the knowledge that in thirty short days she would have a home.

The minute she was back in her suite, she grabbed the phone. She knew she had to call Caine, ask him to represent her interests in the settlement or recommend a local real estate lawyer. She needed to choose an insurance company and take out a home owner's policy. She wanted to shop for furniture, to pick out dishes and linens.

And oh, she'd forgotten to measure the windows for the plantation blinds she wanted.

But first she wanted to share her news and excitement.

"Is Mac—Mr. Blade available?" she asked when Mac's assistant answered the phone. "It's Darcy Wallace."

"Hello, Ms. Wallace. I'm sorry, Mr. Blade's in a meeting. May I take a message?"

"Oh…no, thank you. If you could just tell him I called."

She hung up, deflated as the image in her head of driving him out to the house and telling him it was hers faded. It would have to wait.

She buried herself in work instead, pushing herself toward the end of the book. If her luck held and the agent she'd contacted wanted to see more, she intended to be ready.

When two hours had passed and he hadn't returned her call, she resisted the urge to pick up the phone again. She made herself coffee, then spent another hour tweaking an earlier chapter.

When the phone rang, she pounced. "Hello."

"Darcy. Deb said you called earlier."

"Yes. I wondered if you could spare an hour. There's something I want to show you."

There was a hesitation, a humming kind of silence that had her shifting in her chair.

"I'm sorry. I'm tied up here." In his office Mac sat at his desk and realized the first step away was the hardest. "I'm not going to have any time for you."

"Oh. You must be busy."

"I am. If anything's wrong I can send the hotel manager or the concierge up."

"No, nothing's wrong." The cool formality of his voice made her shudder. "Nothing at all. It can wait. If you have time tomorrow…"

"I'll let you know."

"All right."

"I have to go. Talk to you later."

She stared at the phone in her hand for several seconds before replacing it slowly on the hook. He'd seemed so distant, so different. Hadn't that been mild irritation in his voice, an underlying impatience?

No, she was imagining things. Finding her hands gripped tightly together, she swore at herself and separated them.

He was just busy, she told herself. She'd interrupted his work. People hated to be interrupted. It was her own sense of disappointment—which was foolish—that was making her overreact to a very natural incident.

He'd spent the whole of last evening with her, she remembered, had made wild, almost desperate love to her under the stars. No one could need a woman so much in the night then flick her off like a pesky gnat the next day.

Of course they could, she admitted and pressed her fingers to her eyes. It was naive, even stupid to pretend it couldn't and didn't happen.

But not with Mac. He was too kind, too honest. And she loved him far, far too much.

He was just busy, she insisted. She'd taken up huge amounts of his time over the past two weeks. Naturally he would need to catch up, to concentrate on business, to take some breathing room.

She wasn't going to sulk about it. Darcy straightened her shoulders, tucked the chair back in place. She would concentrate on work herself, and take advantage of what was going to be a long, solitary evening.

She worked for another six hours, remembering to turn on the lights only when she realized she was working in the dark. She drained the pot of coffee and found herself stunned when she came to the end of her book.

Finished. Beginning, middle and end. It was all there now, she thought giddily, all inside this clever little machine and copied onto a small slim disc.

To celebrate she opened a bottle of champagne, though it was a bit of a struggle, and drank an entire glass. With reckless abandon she poured a second and took it to the desk with her to start refining the draft.

She put in twelve hours and went through half a bottle of the wine, which she counteracted with more coffee. It was hardly a wonder that when she finally tumbled into bed she was chased by odd and jumbled dreams.

She saw herself in the tower of her new house, alone. All alone and crowded there by mountains of papers and an enormous computer. Through the window she could see dozens of scenes flip by, like a fast forward through a movie. Parties and people, children playing, couples embracing. The noise—laughter and music—was muffled by the glass that surrounded her.

When she pounded on it, no one heard her. No one saw her. No one cared.

She was in the casino, sitting at the blackjack table. But she couldn't add up her cards, couldn't calculate the math. Didn't know what to do.

Hit or stand. Serena, elegant in a mannish tux watched her impassively. *Hit or stand,* she repeated. *You have to make the choice, then deal with it.*

She doesn't know how to play. Mac stepped up beside her, gave her a brotherly pat on the head. *You don't know the rules, do you?*

But she did, she did. It was just that she couldn't seem to add the cards. There was so much at stake. Didn't they understand how much was at stake?

Never bet more than you can afford to lose, Mac told her with a cool smile. *The house always has the edge.*

Then she was alone again, stumbling along the arrow-straight road through the desert and the lights and colors of Vegas were trapped behind the rippling waves of heat, floating there. No matter how far she walked she couldn't get any closer.

Dust rose in a cloud as Mac drove up, his hair streaming in the wind. *You're going in the wrong direction.*

But she wasn't. She was going home.

He reached out, touched her cheek in an absent, avuncular gesture that made her cringe. *You don't belong here.*

"Yes, I do." Her own furious shout woke her. Sitting up in bed she was stunned by the raw and genuine extent of her anger. She seethed with it, forced herself to take deep, calming breaths.

The sun was bright on her face because she'd forgotten to draw the drapes the night before.

"No more bedtime champagne for you, Darcy," she muttered, rubbing her face as if to rub away the edges of the dreams.

Noting it was already nine, she gave in to impulse and grabbed the phone. Serena answered on the second ring.

"It's Darcy. I hope I'm not calling too early."

"No. Justin and I are just having our first cup of coffee."

"Are you busy today?"

"I don't have to be. What did you have in mind?"

Darcy stood back, nervously twisting her fingers as Serena walked through the first floor of the house.

"I know this might seem sudden," Darcy began. "It's the only one I looked at. But I had a picture in my head of what I wanted, and this… this was even better than that."

"It's…" Serena turned a last circle, then smiled. "Beautiful. It suits you so well. I think you've made a perfect choice."

"Really? Really?" Swamped with joy, Darcy steepled her hands at her mouth. "I was afraid you'd think I was crazy."

"There's nothing crazy about wanting a home of your own, or investing in excellent property."

"Oh, I wanted to show someone so badly. I raced back yesterday as soon as I'd signed the contract. I wanted to show Mac, but he was busy, and well…"

She moved her shoulders and stepped away before she could see Serena's troubled frown. As far as Serena knew, her son hadn't been any busier the day before than normal.

"You told him you bought a house, but he didn't have time to come out and take a look?"

"No, I just told him there was something I wanted him to see. I guess it's silly, but I wanted him to see it first. Please don't tell him about it."

"No, I won't. Darcy, why did you decide to buy a house here, in Vegas?"

"That." Her response was instant as she walked over to the doorway to gaze out at the desert. "It pulls at me. For some people it's water, for some it's mountains, or it's big, bustling cities. For me it's the desert. I had no idea until I got here, and then I knew."

Glowing with pleasure, she turned back. "And I love the Strip, the fantasy of it, the magic and the snap in the air that says anything can happen. Everything does happen. Everybody needs a place, don't you think, that makes them believe they could accomplish something there? Even if it's nothing more than being happy."

"Yes, I do think that, and I'm glad you found it." Still she crossed the room, brushed a hand over Darcy's hair. "But it has to do with Mac, too, doesn't it?" When Darcy didn't answer, Serena smiled softly. "Darling. I can see how you feel about him."

"I can't help being in love with him."

"Of course, you can't. Why should you? But is the house for him, Darcy?"

"It could be," she murmured. "But it's for me first. It has to be. I need a home. I need a place. That's what I'm doing here. I know I can't expect him to feel about me the way I do about him. But I'm willing to gamble. If I lose, at least I'll know I played the game. No more watching from behind the window," she murmured.

"My money's on you."

Darcy's grin flashed like sunlight. "I ought to tell you that I've fallen in love with Mac's family, too."

"Oh, baby." Serena wrapped her close, rubbing cheeks, and reminded herself she hadn't raised any idiots. Mac would come to his senses soon. "Show me the rest of the house."

"Yes, and I was hoping you could go with me to look at furniture."

"I thought you'd never ask."

Darcy was glad to be busy, to have so many details juggling for space in her mind. Colors, fabrics, lamps. Should she convert the smallest bedroom into a library or would the downstairs den suit that purpose best?

Did she want ficus trees flanking the doorway on the main level, or palms?

Every decision was monumentally important to her, and a giddy delight.

Though she yearned to share them all with Mac, they'd had no time alone together for two days.

He was putting all his efforts into keeping his mind occupied and off her. Time, he'd decided, and space, were what both of them needed to ease back far enough and analyze their relationship.

He missed her miserably.

Freedom was undoubtedly what she needed, he told himself. He paced his office, giving up on the idea of work. She hadn't called him again, and from the information he'd discreetly drawn from the staff, she'd been spending nearly as much time out of the hotel as in it.

Flexing those fairy wings, he imagined.

He hadn't let her do that, not really. He'd carried her along, deluding himself initially that he was helping her, then justifying the rest because he'd wanted her.

And still wanted her.

She'd come into his life lost and wounded and desperate for affection. He'd taken advantage of that. It hardly mattered what his motives were, the results were the same.

He imagined she believed herself in love with him. The idea had crossed his mind more than once to take advantage of that as well. To keep her for himself. To see that she went on believing it as long as possible.

After all, she had no experience. No man had touched her before he had touched her. She'd tumbled from a sheltered existence into a dazzling fantasy world. He could sweep her along in that world, keep her dazzled. And his.

It would be easy. And unforgivable.

He cared far too much to trap her, to clip those wings and watch the innocence tarnish. Her life was just beginning, he reminded himself. And his was already set.

Then she burst into his office, her eyes huge, her cheeks wax pale. "I'm sorry. I'm sorry, I know you're busy. I know I shouldn't disturb you, but—but—"

"What is it? Are you hurt?" He had his hands on her in one thumping heartbeat.

"No, no." She shook her head frantically, clutched at his shirt. "I'm okay. No, I'm not okay. I don't know what I am. I sold my book. I sold my book. Sold it. Oh God, I'm dizzy."

"Sold it? Take slow breaths, come on, slow and deep. that's it. I thought the book wasn't finished."

"The other one. The one—last year. She said

the new one, too. Both of them." Giving up, she dropped her forehead to his chest. "I need a minute. I can't think straight." Then she jerked her head up again, laughing wildly. "It's like sex. Maybe I should have a cigarette."

"Have a seat instead."

"No, I can't sit down. I'd bounce right off the chair. They bought the book, no, the books. Two-book contract. Can you imagine? I beat the odds. Again."

"Who bought the book, Darcy? And how?"

"Oh, okay." She gulped in another breath. "A few days ago I got a call from an editor in New York. Eminence Publishing. She'd seen me on the news, and she asked me to send her some of my work."

"A few days ago?" The stab of disappointment was sharp and sudden. "You never mentioned it."

"I wanted to wait until I had an answer. Boy, have I got one now." She pressed her fingers to her eyes as tears swam close. "I'm not going to cry, not yet. I picked an agent off my list. I knew the publisher only wanted to see my work because of the publicity, but there was a chance they'd like it. So I hired an agent."

"Over the phone."

"Yes." The obvious disapproval in his tone made her sigh. "I know it was risky, but I didn't want to wait. The agent called this morning and said they'd made an offer, a very decent offer. Then she advised me to turn it down."

As if that part were just sinking in, Darcy pressed a hand to her stomach. "I couldn't believe it. I had a chance like this, what I've wanted all my life, and she said to say no."

"Why?"

"That's what I asked her. She said…" Darcy closed her eyes, reliving the moment. "She said I had a strong talent, that I told a powerful story, and they were going to have to pay more for it. If they balked, she told me she would take the book to auction. She believed in me. So I took the chance. Ten minutes ago, they bought them both. Now I think I'll sit down."

She all but slid into a chair.

"I'm so happy for you, Darcy." He crouched in front of her. "So proud of you."

"All my life I wanted this. No one ever believed in me." She let the tears come now. "'Be sensible, Darcy. Keep your feet on the ground.' And I always was. I always did because I never thought I was good enough for more."

"You're good enough for anything," he murmured. "More than good enough."

She shook her head. "I always wanted to be. When I was in school, I worked so hard. Both my parents were teachers, and I knew how important it was to them. But no matter how much I put into it, I brought home B's instead of A's. They'd look at my report card, and there'd be this silent little sigh. They'd tell me I'd done well, but I could do better if I just worked harder. I couldn't do better. Just couldn't. It was the best I could do, but it was never good enough."

"They were wrong."

"They didn't mean to be so critical. They just didn't understand." Wanting the anchor, she held tight to his hands. "I used to show them the stories I'd write, just once wanting them to be impressed, enthusiastic. It just wasn't in them, so I stopped showing them. And I stopped looking for their approval, at least outwardly."

She sighed, wiped at her face with her fingers.

"I never sent off the first book. Couldn't find the courage to. I suppose inside I was always hoping, waiting for someone to tell me I was good enough. Now I've done it, and someone has."

"Here." He pulled a handkerchief out of his pocket and pressed it into her hands.

"I'm not sad." She sniffled, mopped at her face. "There's just so much going on inside me. So many things have been happening. I had to tell you."

"I'm glad you did. News like this can't wait." He framed her face in his hands, and after a brief internal struggle, pressed his lips to her forehead rather than her mouth. "We'll have to celebrate." He let his hands linger on her face a moment, then dropped them and rose. "We'll get together for drinks and you can tell me your plans."

"Plans?"

"You'll want to fly into New York for a few days, I imagine. Meet your publisher, your agent."

"Yes, maybe next week."

So soon, he thought and suffered as he looked down at her tear-streaked face and made the break. "You'll be missed around here," he said lightly. "I hope you'll keep in touch, let us know where you settle."

"Settle. But…I'm coming back here."

"Here?" He lifted a brow, then smiled. "Darcy, as delighted as we've been to have you, you can't keep living in a high roller's suite." He laughed a little and sat on the edge of his desk. "A high roller, you're not. You're more than welcome to stay until you finalize your travel plans."

He was running a business, she thought frantically. She'd been taking advantage of his generosity, occupying an expensive suite for two weeks. "I hadn't thought. I'm sorry. I'll book another room when I get back until—"

"Darcy, there's no reason for you to come back here."

"Of course there is." Her heart began to flutter hard in her throat. "I live here."

"The Comanche's not your home. It's mine." He wasn't smiling now, and his eyes had gone cool and hard. It was the only way he could face the stunned hurt on her face. "It's time for you to start your own life, and you can't do that here.

You've accomplished something really extraordinary. Now enjoy it."

"You don't want me anymore. You're not just kicking me out of your hotel. You're kicking me out of your life."

"No one's kicking you out of anything."

"No?" She managed a half laugh and balled the handkerchief in her fist. "How stupid do you think I am? You've been avoiding me for days. You've barely touched me since I came in the room. Now you're giving me a little pat on the head and telling me to run along and have a nice life."

"I do want you to have a nice life," he began.

"As long as it's somewhere else," she retorted. "Well, that's too bad, because I'm having my life here. I bought a house."

He'd prepared himself for a miserable scene, for tears, for recriminations. But he was stunned speechless. "What? You bought what?"

"I bought a house."

"Have you lost your mind? A house? Here? What were you thinking of?"

"Myself. It's a new concept for me and I like it."

"You don't buy a damn house the way you do a new dress."

"I'm not the bubble-brain you apparently think I am. I know how to buy a house, and I've done it."

"You have no business buying a house in Vegas."

"Oh really?" Her emotions were careering so fast she didn't know how her words could keep pace. "Do you own the entire city and its environs now? Well, I seem to have found the one little spot you don't have control over. I like it here, and I'm staying."

"Life is not an endless cruise down the Strip."

"And Vegas is not only the Strip. It's the fastest growing city in the country, and one of the most livable. It has an excellent school system, job opportunities abound and the housing is very affordable. Water's a problem, and that's an issue that's going to have to be seriously addressed in the near future. However, the crime rate is markedly low in comparison with other major cities and the area's continuing ability to reinvent itself gives it high marks for potential into the next century."

She paused, her eyes glittering when he said nothing. "I'm a writer. I was a librarian. I damn well know how to research."

"Did your research mention how many pawn-shops are in Vegas per square mile? Did it touch on prostitution, corruption, money laundering, gambling addictions?"

"Actually, it did," she said evenly now. "Sin exists. It may shock you to know I was aware of it before I came here."

"You simply haven't thought this through."

"You're wrong. Absolutely wrong. I didn't buy this house blind, and I didn't buy it so I could keep falling at your feet. I bought it for me," she said fiercely. "Because I found something I always wanted and never expected to have. But don't worry, Vegas is big enough so that I won't get in your way."

"Wait a minute. Damn it," he muttered, and put a hand on her shoulder to turn her. But she spun around, lifting both hands with a look in her eye that warned him to keep his distance.

"Don't. I don't need placating, and I don't intend to cause a scene. I'm grateful to you, and

I don't want to forget that. I fully intend to have a relationship with your parents, your family and don't want to put them, or you, in a position that makes that difficult. But you hurt me," she said quietly. "And you didn't have to."

She walked to the door, shut it firmly behind her.

Chapter Twelve

"So we agree to forgive two million of Harisuki and Tanaka's baccarat losses." Justin lounged in the wide leather chair, pretending he didn't notice his son's inattention. "That puts them into the casino for ten and twelve million respectively. We comp the rooms, the meals, the bar bills and cover their wives' spending spree in the boutique. They'll be back," he said, drawing idly on his cigar. "And they'll drop the next several million right here instead of across the street. You arranged for the limo for them tomorrow?" He waited a beat. "Mac?"

"What? Yes. It's taken care of."

"Good. Now that we've finished all that up, you can tell me what's on your mind."

"Nothing in particular. Do you want a beer?"

Justin indicated assent with a wave of his hand. "We always had to pry problems out of you. Your determination to handle everything yourself is admirable, but it's annoying." He smiled cheerfully at his son and accepted the cold brown bottle. "However, in this case, prying isn't necessary—trouble with Darcy."

"No. Yes. No," Mac repeated, and blew out a breath. "She sold her book. Actually she sold two books."

"That's wonderful. She must be thrilled. Why aren't you?"

"I am. I'm happy for her. It's what she's always wanted. I don't think I realized how much she wanted it. This will give her a whole new direction."

"Is that what's worrying you? She won't need you anymore?"

"No. The whole issue is for her to move ahead

with her life. This was just some breathing space for her."

"Was it? Mac, are you in love with her?"

"That's not the point."

"It's the only point that counts."

"I'm wrong for her. This place is wrong for her." Restless, he stalked to the window, staring out at the carnival of neon and colored fountains. "Once she focuses she'll see that."

"Why are you wrong for her? It seemed to me you complemented each other very well."

"I run a casino. My peak hours are when sensible people are tucked into their beds." He jammed his hands into his pockets. "She's lived a sheltered life. More, a repressed one where she's been held back, held down. She's just starting to realize what she can do and be and have. I don't have any right to interfere with that."

"You're making this black-and-white, sinner and saint. I don't think either of you qualify. You're a businessman, and a good one. She's an interesting, refreshingly enthusiastic young woman."

"Who walked in here a few weeks ago," Mac

reminded him. "A few weeks ago and at a turning point in her life. She can't possibly know what her feelings are."

"You underestimate her. But regardless, aren't your own feelings important?"

"I've already let my feelings take over more than once. She walked in here untouched." Mac turned back, his eyes swirling and dark. "I changed that. I should have kept my hands off her, but I didn't. I couldn't."

"Now you're going to punish yourself for being human," Justin concluded. "You're going to deny yourself a relationship that makes you happy, and your reasoning is she'll be better off."

"She's dazzled," Mac insisted, wondering why saying it all out loud this way made it sound so wrong and so foolish. "And only seeing what she wants to see. She bought a house, for God's sake."

"Yes, I know."

"And—you know." Mac stared at his father.

"She took your mother to see it the day after she signed the contract. I went to see it myself. It's a fine piece of property, an intriguing, attractive home."

"It's ludicrous to buy a house in a place you've only been for a few weeks, and when you've spent most of that time in a hotel casino. She's living in a fantasy land."

"No, she's not. She knows exactly what she wants, and I'm surprised you don't realize that. If you don't want her, that's a different matter."

"I can't stop wanting her." It was like an ache that couldn't be eased. "I was sure I could."

"Wanting's easy. The first time I saw your mother I wanted her. That was as natural as breathing. But loving her terrified me. Sometimes it still does."

Surprised, Mac lowered to a chair. "You make that part look easy, too. You always have. You're so…matched," he decided.

"Is that the problem?" Justin leaned over, put his hand over Mac's.

"No, not a problem. It's just that marriages work in our family. The odds are against it, but they work for us." He studied the gold band on his father's finger. Thirty years, he thought, and it still fit. That was a kind of miracle. "I figure they work because we're careful to find a mate—in the literal sense of the word. A match."

"You're seeing your mother and I as a set, something that came that way. It's not true. We were a half-breed ex-con who'd gotten lucky and the privileged daughter of wealthy, indulgent parents. Long odds, Mac, on a pair like that."

"But you were heading in the same direction."

Justin leaned back again, eyes sharp. "The hell we were. What we did was beat a new path, and there were plenty of bumps along the way."

"You're telling me I've made a mistake," Mac murmured. "And maybe you're right." He ran his hand over his face. "I'm not sure anymore."

"You want guarantees? There aren't any. Loving a woman's the riskiest game in town. You either put up your stake, or you back away from the table. But if you back away, you never win. Is she the woman you want?"

"Yes."

"I'll ask you again. Are you in love with her?"

"Yes." Admitting it intensified the ache. "And yes, it's terrifying."

Sympathizing, Justin smiled. "What do you want to do about it."

"I want her back." He let out a long breath. "I've got to get her back."

"How bad have you screwed it up?"

"Pretty bad." It made him slightly ill to realize just how poorly he'd played his hand. "I all but shoved her out the door."

"It may take some fast talk to get her to open her side of that door again."

"So I'll talk fast." Misery vanished in a spurt of reckless energy. It was a new hand, he thought, fresh cards. And everything he had was going into the pot. "I'd better go down and try to work this out with her. She must be sitting in her room, miserable, when she should be out celebrating."

"I think you lose on that one," Justin murmured, studying the screens.

"There's a pair of star-shaped diamond earrings in the jewelry store downstairs." Mac checked his pocket to make certain he had his passkey for the elevator. Just in case. "She should have something special to celebrate selling her book."

He was suddenly nervous, a sensation he

wasn't accustomed to. "Do you think the earrings and flowers are overkill?"

Justin ran his tongue around his teeth. "I don't think you can ever overkill in a situation like this. But…you're not going to find Darcy in her room."

"Hmm?"

"You better take a look. Screen three, second craps table from the left."

Anxious to be on his way, Mac glanced absently at the screen. Then looked again. His wounded fairy was decked out in that little killer of a red dress with spiked heels to match, and was blowing on a pair of dice.

"What the hell is she doing?"

"Going for an eight. That's her point. Five and a three," he said, and grinned when he heard his son slam the door on his way out. "The lady wins."

"Come on, baby. Come on, doll. Bring it home."

The man cheering beside Darcy was old enough to be her father, so she didn't mind the little pat he gave her butt. She took it as a good-luck wish.

She shook the dice in her hand, leaned over the

long table and let them fly. Cheers roared out, and money and chips changed hands too quickly for her to follow.

"Seven! All right." She pumped a fist in the air. After raking in her pile of chips, she began recklessly distributing them again. "This on the point, and this, um, behind. Five's my point."

"Roll 'em, blondie." The man on the other side of her plunked a hundred-dollar bill on the table. "You're hot."

"Damn right I am." She sent the dice tumbling, squinting through the smoke, and howled with triumph when the ivories came up three and two.

"I don't know why I thought this game was so hard." She grinned then gulped from the fresh glass of champagne someone handed her. "Hold this, will you?" She shoved the glass at the butt-patter and picked up the dice. "Let mine ride," she told the croupier. "God, I *love* saying that!" She tossed the dice, then danced on three-inch heels.

Mac had to elbow his way through a crowd gathered four deep. His first sight of her was a tight little butt molded into clinging red. He caught her elbow just after her toss, and his words were swallowed by the roar of players and onlookers.

"What the hell do you think you're doing?"

She tossed back her head, drunk on victory. "I'm kicking your ass. Back up and give me room so I can kick it some more."

He snagged her wrist as she leaned over to scoop up the dice. "Cash in."

"The hell I will. I'm smoking."

"Come on, pal, let the lady roll."

Mac merely turned his head and iced down the eager player on the corner of the table with a look. "Cash her in," he ordered the croupier, then dragged Darcy through the bitter complaints of the crowd.

"You can't make me stop playing when I'm on a streak."

"You're wrong. This is my place, and I can make anybody stop playing anytime. The house has the edge."

"Fine." She jerked her arm free. "I'll take my business elsewhere, and I'm let them know the management at The Comanche can't hold up under a run of honest luck."

"Darcy, come upstairs. We need to talk."

"Don't tell me what I need to do." She pulled away again sharply, almost pleased when heads turned and attention zeroed in on them. "I told you I wouldn't cause a scene, but I will if you push me. You can kick me out of your casino, and you can kick me out of your hotel, but you can't tell me what I need to do."

"I'm asking you," he said with what he considered amazing patience, "to come with me so we can discuss this privately."

"And I'm telling you, I'm not interested."

"Okay, the hard way." He scooped her up and over his shoulder. He'd taken ten strides before she broke through the shock and began to struggle.

"Let go of me. You can't treat me this way."

"You made your choice," he said grimly, and ignored the stunned looks of guests and staff as he carted her to the elevator.

"I don't want to talk to you. I'm already packed. I'm leaving in the morning. Just let me go."

"The hell I will." He keyed in her floor, then dumped her back on her feet. "You've got a stubborn streak in you, and I'm—" He broke off when her fist punched into his stomach. It didn't do much more than bounce off and cause him to lift a coolly amused brow.

"We'll have to work on that."

Conceding that she was outgunned, Darcy folded her arms. When the doors opened into her suite, she sailed out. "This may be your place, but this is my room until morning, and I don't want you in it."

"We need to straighten things out."

"Things are perfectly straight, thank you just the same."

"Darcy, you don't understand."

She shoved away the hands he'd laid on her shoulders. "That's just it, isn't it? You don't think I understand anything. You think I'm a fluff-brained idiot who doesn't know how to take care of herself."

"I don't think you're an idiot."

"But fluff-brained just the same," she countered. "Well, I'm sharp enough to know that you got tired of me and your solution was to brush me off like an irritating child."

"Tired of you?" At the end of his rope, he

dragged his hands through his hair. "I know I made a mess of it. Let me explain."

"There's nothing to explain. You don't want me. Fine. I'm not going to jump off a roof over it." She jerked a shoulder and turned away. "I'm young, I'm rich, I have my career to think of. And you're not the only man in the world."

"Just a damn minute."

"You were the first." She shot a searing look over her shoulder. "That doesn't mean you have to be the last."

Which had been one of his points. Exactly one of the reasons he'd been so determined to step away. But hearing it from her, seeing that hot, female look in her eyes had a rage bubbling up in him so violently it hazed his vision.

"Watch your step, Darcy."

"I've watched it all my life, and I'm finished. I like leaping before I look. And so far I'm landing on my feet. If and when I fall it'll be my problem and no one else's."

Panic skidded up his spine because he could see she meant it. She could do it, would do it. "You know damn well you're in love with me."

Her heart toppled and cracked. "Because I slept with you? Please."

However derisive her words, her fingers had linked together and twisted. It was just enough of a tell for him to call her bluff. "You wouldn't have slept with me if you hadn't been in love with me. If I held you right now. If I put my mouth on yours, you'd tell me without saying a word."

Every defense crumbled. "You knew, and you used it."

"Maybe I did. I've had a hard time with that, and made more mistakes because I couldn't get past it."

"Are you guilty or angry, Mac?" Wearily she turned away again. "You broke my heart. I'd have given it to you on a platter. It wasn't even enough for you not to want it, you ignored it."

"I told myself I was doing it for you."

"For me." A laugh choked out. "Well, that was considerate of you."

"Darcy." He reached out, but her shoulders rounded as she cringed away. An ache sliced through him as he dropped his hands again. "I won't touch you, but at least look at me."

"What do you want from me? Do you want me to say it's all right? That I understand. I won't hold it against you. It's not all right." Her breath hitched in a sob that was brutal to control. "I don't understand, and I'm trying not to hold it against you. You weren't obligated to feel what I felt—that was my gamble. But in the end you could have been kind."

"If I'd trusted my feelings, we wouldn't be having this conversation. And I don't want to have it here." When a hunch came this sudden and strong, he knew to ride it out. "I want to see your house."

"What?"

"I'd like very much to see your house. Now."

"Now?" She passed a hand over her eyes. "It's late. I'm tired. I don't have the keys."

"What's the name of the realtor? Do you have a card?"

"Yes, on the desk. But—"

"Good."

To her confusion he walked to the phone, dialed the number and in less than two minutes was on a first-name basis with Marion Baines and jotting down her address.

"She'll give us the keys," Mac told Darcy when he hung up. "Shouldn't take more than twenty minutes to get to her place."

"You're a powerful man," she said dryly. "What's the point of this?"

"Take a chance." He smiled in challenge. "Leap before you look. Do you want a jacket?"

She refused one, and would have refused to go with him if she hadn't wanted one scrap of pride to take with her. They didn't speak. She thought that was best. Perhaps, somehow, this quiet drive would settle the nerves and let them part—if not as friends—with some respect for each other.

He seemed to know his way. He picked up the keys without incident, then easily wove toward the outskirts where her house stood, a soft silhouette under the slowly waning moon.

"Trust you," he murmured, scanning the shape. "You found a castle after all."

It nearly made her smile. "That's what I thought when I saw it. That's how I knew it was mine."

"Ask me in."

"You've got the keys," she noted, and opened her door.

He waited until she'd rounded the hood, then held the keys out to her. "Ask me in, Darcy."

She fought the urge to snatch the keys from him, telling herself he was trying to do what he could to make the situation less miserable. She accepted the keys and started up the walk.

"I've never been in it at night. There are flood-lights in both the house and yard."

He thought about her out there, alone, at night. "Is there a security system?"

"Yes, I have the code." She unlocked the door and turned directly to a small box beside it. She disengaged the alarm, then switched on the lights.

He said nothing, but walked through much as his mother had done. But in this case, the silence unnerved her. "I've been looking at furniture, found many pieces that I like."

"It's a lot of space."

"I've discovered I like a lot of space."

She'd put plants on the decks, he imagined. Cheerful pots full of lush green and delicate blossoms she'd baby. She'd want soft colors inside, cool and soothing, with the occasional flash to shake things up.

It amazed him how clearly he could imagine it, and how easy it was to know her after so little time.

He switched on the outside lights and watched them flood the blue water of the pool and the rippling sea of the desert beyond.

It was stunning, powerful, and in its own way calm as the night sky. Maybe he'd lost sight of this, he mused, this other side of the world from where he'd chosen to live. And because of that, had refused to accept her place there.

"This is what you want."

"Yes. This is what I want."

"The tower. You'll write there."

She ached a little, because he would know. "Yes."

"We never celebrated." He turned back. She was standing in the center of the empty room, her hands linked, her eyes shadowed. "My fault. I need you to know, Darcy, how happy I am for you, and how sorry I am I spoiled the moment."

Guilt, she thought. He was too kind a man not to feel it. "It doesn't matter."

"It matters," he corrected. "A great deal. I'd like to try to explain. I'd like you to try to see it from my viewpoint. You fell into my arms, literally, the first time I saw you. You were alone, lonely, a little desperate, completely vulnerable and impossibly appealing. I wanted you too much, too quickly. I'm good at resisting temptation, that's why I'm good at what I do. But I couldn't resist you."

"You didn't seduce me, you didn't force me. It was a mutual attraction."

"But it wasn't an even hand." He stepped toward her, relieved when she didn't back away. "I took you because I wanted you, because I could, because I needed to, knowing you'd want and need more. Deserved more. But I didn't intend to give it to you."

"It was a chance I took. You told me flat out, before we were lovers, you didn't have marriage on your mind. I didn't fall in bed with you blindly."

He paused a moment, surprised. "You gambled on me changing my mind?"

"The odds might have been long that you'd fall in love with me, but they weren't infinitesimal." The edge had come back into her voice. "Your grandfather thinks I'm perfect for you. So does your mother."

He very nearly choked. "You talked to my mother?"

"I love your mother," she said passionately. "And I have a perfect right to have someone to talk to."

"I didn't mean it that way. I'm getting off the track," he said with a sigh. "The way I saw it, you needed a little time to settle, to explore the possibilities, to have some fun and indulge yourself. So you'd gamble a little, spend some money, take a few rides. Discover sex."

"So you were what, tutoring me? How much more insulting can you possibly be?"

"I'm not trying to insult you. I'm trying to tell you what I believed, and that I was wrong."

"You haven't begun to say you were wrong yet. Maybe you should get started."

"You've got a nasty streak." He dipped his hands into his pockets. "I never noticed it before."

"I've been saving it up. So the little country mouse comes to the big city and the clever city mouse lets her taste a bit of sin, then shows her the door before she damns her soul to perdition? Is that close enough?"

"A long, wide nasty streak. You were alone and afraid and over your head."

"And you tossed me a float."

"Shut up." Patience straining, he gripped her arms. "Nobody ever gave you a choice. You said so yourself. No one gave you a chance. No one let you bloom. God, Darcy, you've done nothing but bloom since you got here, since you had that chance, that choice. How was I supposed to take that choice away from you? You've never been anywhere else. You've never been with anyone else. I wasn't going to watch you living in a hotel, wandering through a casino, locking yourself to me because you didn't know any better."

"And that's your way of giving me a choice. Funny, that's just the kind of choice people have been giving me all my life."

"I know. I'm sorry."

"So am I." She lifted her hands to his arms and pushed until he released her. "Are we finished?"

"No. Not yet."

"Oh, what's the point of this?" She strode away from him, her sassy shoes clicking on the tiles.

"Why do you want a tour of the place now? Do we pretend we're pals? What are we doing here?"

"I wanted to finish this here because it's not my place. It's yours." He waited until she turned back. "The house always has the advantage."

"I don't know what you're talking about."

"My father told me something tonight I'd never considered. He said wanting is easy, but loving is terrifying." His eyes stayed locked on hers. "You terrify me, Darcy, right down to the bone." He watched as she wrapped her arms tight around her body. "When I look at you, I'm scared senseless."

"Don't do this. It's not fair."

"I tried to be fair, and all I did was hurt you, and make myself miserable. I'm playing a new hand now, and when the house has the edge, I can't afford to play fair. There's no point in backing away," he said when she did just that. "I'll only keep coming after you. You brought this on yourself. I'd have let you go."

He caught her, ran his hands from her shoulders to her wrists then back again. "You're trembling. Scared?" He touched his lips to the corner of hers. "That must mean you still love me."

Her breath was hot in her chest, tangling in her throat. "I won't have you feeling sorry for me. I don't—"

The kiss was sudden and violent. Her heart slammed once, twice, hard against her ribs then began a wild and unsteady beat.

"Is that what you think this is? This feels like pity to you?" He took her mouth again, diving deep. "Damn, this dress drives me crazy. I could have killed every man at that table tonight just for looking at you. I'll have to buy you a dozen more like it."

"You're not making sense. I don't know what you're saying."

"I love you."

This time her heart took one high, joyful leap. "You do?"

"I love everything about you." He lifted her hands, pressed them to his lips, then gently untangled her fingers. "And I'm asking you to buck the odds and give me another chance."

Her lips trembled, then curved. "I'm a big believer in another chance."

"I was counting on it." This time he kissed her

gently, easing her into his arms. "But you're going to have to let me move in here."

"Here?" She was floating, drifting, close to dreaming. "You want to live here?"

"Well, I figure this is where you'll want to raise the kids."

"Kids?" Her dazzled eyes flew open again.

"You want kids, don't you?" He smiled when her head bobbed up and down. "I like big families—and coming from one, I'm a traditionalist. If we're going to make kids together, you have to marry me."

"Mac." It was all she could say, just his name. Nothing else would get through.

"Willing to risk it, Darcy?" He lifted her hands again, pressed them to his heart. "Want to take a gamble on us?"

His heart beat under her hands, and was no steadier than hers. "It so happens," she said with a brilliant smile, "I'm on a hot streak."

He laughed, scooped her off her feet in one wide, dizzying circle. "So I've heard."

* * * * *

Meet Nora Robert's
The MacGregors family

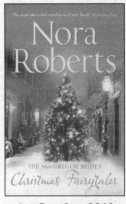

1st October 2010

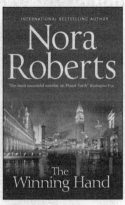

3rd December 2010

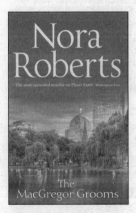

7th January 2011

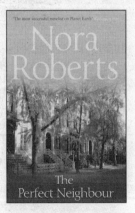

4th February 2011

www.millsandboon.co.uk

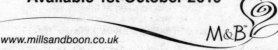

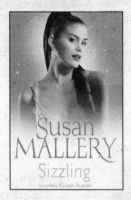